THE RUMOUR MILL

Roxy Jacenko is the powerhouse behind Sydney's hottest fashion, beauty and lifestyle PR firm, Sweaty Betty PR. Not only do the products she publicises make the pages of every magazine in town, but so does Roxy herself. It's rare to see her away from the social pages. She starred in 2013's *Celebrity Apprentice*, and her profile is only going up! Read Roxy's bestselling Jazzy Lou novels, *Strictly Confidential*, and her latest, *The Spotlight*.

THE RUMOUR MILL

A JAZZY LOU NOVEL

ROXY JACENKO

ALLEN&UNWIN
SYDNEY•MELBOURNE•AUCKLAND•LONDON

This is a work of fiction. Whilst a number of real life celebrities are referred to by name in this book, there is no suggestion that any of them were actually involved with any activity or event described in it. All other characters in this book are purely fictional and readers must not assume that any of the events within it are based upon actual facts or real people.

This edition published in 2015
First published in 2013

Allen & Unwin
83 Alexander Street
Crows Nest NSW 2065
Australia
Phone: (61 2) 8425 0100
Email: info@allenandunwin.com
Web: www.allenandunwin.com

Cataloguing-in-Publication details are available
from the National Library of Australia
www.trove.nla.gov.au

ISBN 978 1 76011 137 3

Typeset in Joanna MT Std by Bookhouse, Sydney
Printed in Australia by McPherson's Printing Group

10 9 8 7 6 5 4 3 2 1

MIX
Paper from
responsible sources
FSC® C001695
www.fsc.org

The paper in this book is FSC® certified.
FSC® promotes environmentally responsible,
socially beneficial and economically viable
management of the world's forests.

For my Betties xx

1

Everyone knows that if your waters break at Westfield, Bondi Junction (aka WBJ), the concierge organises a ride for you to hospital and you're entitled to a shopping spree when you're once again able to walk and not waddle. Well, that's the word out there on the street anyway. (If the WBJ story is true, Westfield's billionaire owner, Frank Lowy, must really like the idea of a baby commencing his or her entry into the world surrounded by some of the most expensive designer real estate in the shopping universe. Hell, it's a wonder he doesn't issue the brand-new prospective fashion consumer with a Black Amex credit card right then and there.)

I've never actually met anyone whose waters have broken at WBJ. In fact, I never considered such a majorly embar-rassing moment could happen at all. It's bad enough being pregnant and being mistaken for someone who makes a habit of wearing size 18 clothes without also having to deal with sudden drainage issues – especially when you work in the fashion industry and must pretend that bodily functions do not exist. (Fashionistas do not sweat, visit the WC or eat in public beyond rearranging a few lettuce leaves around on a plate in the restaurant du jour. Sipping a bottle of L'Eau through a straw is acceptable; expelling liquid from any orifice is definitely not.)

But now imagine you're Australia's premier fashion publicist – the owner and chief shit kicker of your own PR consultancy, Queen Bee – and your waters break just before the start of design diva Allison Palmer's show at BMW Fashion Week. Do you pretend to be part of the pre-show entertainment? Or hope no one noticed that it's currently raining from your vajayjay (Water features are so 2003.)

It may have been karma, punishment for my having hooked up with the charming, witty and hot Michael Lloyd, the stockbroker ex-boyfriend of well-seasoned pin-up girl Belle Single. Not that she had probably noticed he had moved on. The wannabe actress and number one ticket holder for the Elouera Beach Car Park (okay, I'm being mean – one of the Sutherland Shire's finest daughters) goes through men just as vigorously as the Cronulla Sharks get through coldies after a game. Her appetite is insatiable, especially if the guy is rich and famous. Michael, sadly, was only filthy rich and wasn't all that keen on seeing his photo front and centre with Belle's in my BFF Luke Jefferson's column in The Sun. Michael and Belle broke up shortly after the action-packed *Coco* Man of the Year Awards, when she had been caught giggling behind a toilet cubicle with Dev – lead singer of The Dread, who had been performing that night. Michael had walked in on them unexpectedly and, well, when he wanted to leave straight away I organised him an Uber car from the event, but I managed to jump in as well. Michael had been excellent company for me during the night, keeping me calm and pouring the odd drink for me while Belle flitted around. Once it was clear that he and Belle were over for good, I accidentally on purpose found myself running into him all over town. It was only a matter of time before we started dating and we were now desperately in love. He really was my knight in shining Armani, my saviour in Paul Smith – in fact, my perfectly groomed accessory.

We could trace the moment of conception with some precision to a delicious weekend break to Qualia on the Great Barrier Reef. It was easy to work out the date because it was one of the rare occasions when we'd had time away from our busy schedules to devote to sex, and lots of it. We'd turned off our phones, declined to glance at our email alerts and not once fired up our social media accounts, and wallowed in this extracurricular activity. When we staggered back to reality at the end of the weekend, slightly the worse for wear and with absolutely no sign of a tan to show for our island break, I had the feeling that something had shifted inside me, but I'd put it down to too much room-service food. I just never dreamt that it would be anything as monumental as a baby. It would be another six weeks before I knew for sure, and by that time I'd already started to plan the mini wardrobe. As you do.

If you really want to know, I thought I was infertile, but it turned out it was only my schedule that had acted as a contraceptive. The timing had never been right before, but this time the planets must have been aligned (and I had been seeing stars in my eyes). Michael was going to make the most perfect dad.

Now here I was nearly nine months later, during the busiest time of the year for Queen Bee – BMW Sydney Fashion Week – and I had no sooner clapped eyes on Belle Single herself walking arm in arm with my nemesis and old PR boss, Diane Wilderstein, than I started to feel a very odd sensation.

You could hardly blame my baby for arcing up on my behalf: the two of them were trying to talk their way into Allison Palmer's evening wear show in a bid to snare one of the coveted front-row seats just minutes before the runway was due to light up. They had no doubt been counting on some of the kosher celebrities not showing up. Unfortunately for them, Diane was no longer such a force in the industry. Call me conceited, but her business started to unravel five years ago when she threw me out after I had been almost sexually assaulted by Gen X cricketing legend Matt Ashley; and it was all captured in The Sun's gossip pages the next day. The problem was that the client, Lacoste, had not been happy because Matt Ashley had looked anything but classy in their polo shirt. Like that was my fault? Diane had nevertheless done me a favour in forcing me to open my own agency, and then slowly but surely I had relieved her of her best accounts. She was seldom even referred to as Cruella De Vil now – more likely just one of the dalmatians.

At the same time, Belle Single's media currency had bombed almost as dramatically as Greece's credit rating; even *Pillow Talk*, her late-night talk show on Channel 42 where, lingerie-clad, she interviewed various identities, had been largely unwatched. Admittedly, she still looked her best when barely dressed, but her interview technique was mind-numbingly dull. The main advantage of having it on so late at night was that it sent most of its viewers to sleep.

Had I not been in the throes of early labour I would have marched right up to Belle and Diane and told them in no uncertain terms to hit the road. But due to the fact that I was currently impersonating Niagara Falls, I was hardly in a position to sort it all out. Luckily my hard-working Bees are always on Belle alert, so before you could say 'skanky blonde' she was quickly ushered into Row C. Those scuffed Prada heels of hers hardly touched the ground.

'But I never do Row C,' I heard her squeak in horror, before meekly sitting down in her assigned spot. It was either Row C or Row Z, which wasn't even inside the tent.

As for that poisonous PR vixen Diane Wilderstein, it would be standing room only. Those ever-present Dior shades clamped on her head (to give her hair the body that her hairdresser could not) were going to get quite a workout today. She would really be hoping that nobody recognised her. Unfortunately, this was unlikely; she was practically a poster gal for Botox gone bad.

'Don't you know who I am? I could break you in this town,' she snarled at poor, hapless Kimmy, one of Queen Bee's newly minted junior publicists.

'S-s-sorry,' stammered Kimmy, who looked like she was about to shit herself, 'but we're over capacity.'

I noted with some satisfaction the look of utter distaste on Diane's face as she was shown to the back of the room by our newest recruit. Diane would have to share the space with hordes of fashion students and assorted hangers-on who were immune to the indignity of hovering at Fashion Week. In her trademark Chanel suit, Wilderstein looked quite ridiculous among them all. If I was her, I would have gone home.

Unfortunately, there wasn't a moment to savour this victory – it was all about what was happening to me right now. When I had first felt a slight trickle, I had distractedly assumed I was having a period. Then it registered: it couldn't be that time of the month since I was so huge that I made Demi Moore in that famous pregnant pose on the cover of *Vanity Fair* magazine look like Victoria Beckham.

My baby, codenamed Project B among the Bees, was well and truly cooked and appeared to be arriving one week ahead of its due date. Well, of course, no child of mine was ever going to miss a deadline. My Allison Palmer sequined dress wasn't exactly what I'd been planning to wear to hospital for the big event (it was going to be some Céline limited-edition sport luxe trousers). I looked like a giant Christmas bauble, and that pair of Madonna-ish headphones clamped around my Valonz blowdry just set the whole thing off, in a really bad way.

'Code 3, Code 3 – is anyone listening?' I hissed into the walkie-talkie when the full horror of my situation dawned on me. I knew the top-secret code would bring the Bees running, and I needed to have my driver sent around to the back of the models' dressing room. There was enough action due to take place on the runway with the models enacting being at a cocktail party without me adding to it in all my amniotic fluid-saturated glory.

It was almost too late to make an exit because Henri – the former male model who was Fashion Week's seating Nazi – was ordering the plastic cover rolled off the runway, and Allison's models were lining up behind the stage. If I bolted for the back door I risked upending one and breaking her neck as she fell off her Givenchy heels.

Just then I spotted super-catty gossip columnist Wally Grimes sashaying towards me with a big fake smile on his lips. 'Quick!' I shouted to Lulu and the rest of the Bees, who were also making their way through the crowd towards me. Just before Wally could pounce, my team surrounded me in the flying wedge formation we had rehearsed just for Code 3 situations, and we moved as one towards the backstage area, which was still a scene of chaos.

Front and centre was Marron, Australia's most famous makeup artist, in head-to-toe Tom Ford, being filmed touching up supermodel Laetitia Leighton, who would not make her special entrance until halfway through the show. The crowd would be on the edge of their seats, almost ravenous with anticipation for her big moment, especially as her well-known actor boyfriend, Nick Rees, was due to be seated just before the lights went down (or, worst-case scenario, in one of the moments of darkness during the show). The fashion editors would be beside themselves: Laetitia's fashion moment was more keenly anticipated than the arrival of the latest Céline It Bag from Paris. Even the usually unflappable Marron was all aquiver as he explained for the TV cameras exactly the look he was going for on the runway. His artfully made-up eyes widened a little when he took in the moving mass of Bees surrounding me, but luckily he had been around fashion shows long enough not to be surprised by anything he saw backstage.

He blew me a big, theatrical kiss. 'Jazzy darling, you look divine! We simply must catch up, but right now I'm giving an interview to Tara Robinson for Six Nightly News,' he announced unnecessarily, as if I didn't recognise Tara or know what was going on. I'd actually locked in the backstage interview.

'Of course,' I responded, air-kissing back in his general direction. 'I understand completely – maybe after the show?' Never let it be said that I don't continue to play my role as an uber-publicist even in the most confronting of circumstances. Lulu shot me a quizzical look. Did I really think I was going to be back in time for the after-party?

'Great, darling, we'll have a glass of bubbles soon. Can't wait,' Marron called back, not noticing that anything was amiss with the massively pregnant woman who was all but being carried out in front of him. All these civilities were exhausting when my body was turning against me – who knew what was going to happen next? Would Project B arrive before we had even left Fashion Week? When it came to hot messes, I was up there with the best of them.

When we were finally sitting in the back of the car with the driver, a wad of Fashion Wipes beside me on the back seat in case of further spillage, I asked, 'Is Michael meeting us at the hospital, Lulu?' completely forgetting that he was on a business trip to China and not merely lunching in Chinatown. In all the chaos I hadn't had a chance to call Michael myself, so Lulu had managed to get through to him on a pre-arranged number in Beijing shortly after I hit the walkie-talkies. He told her that he would be on the next plane out. That's BMW Fashion Week for you: it can sweep you off your feet and make you overlook the really important things in life – like having a baby.

🍸

So this is what labour feels like – no big deal at all, I mused, convinced that if my waters had broken I must be in labour, and yet I didn't feel a twinge of pain. I'd had headaches and stomach ulcers worse than this.

Perhaps if I had attended one of the birth information sessions run by the Prince of Wales Private Hospital I might have been across the various stages of giving birth, but I could never fit them into the Queen Bee schedule. I couldn't lit anything much into the Queen Bee schedule. It had pretty much developed a life of its own.

'Quick, Lulu, look up "stages of labour" in Wikipedia,' I pleaded, and my loyal assistant immediately typed rapidly on the screen of her BlackBerry. She took a moment or two to read it and try to digest it all.

'Do you think you're dilated yet?' she asked. 'Has the baby's head engaged?'

Her words were making me feel as squeamish as one of the more realistic episodes of CSI. 'What? Lulu, I'm not sure I can do this,' I said with a touch of panic.

'I don't think you have a choice,' she said kindly. 'That baby is busting to be born.'

But before I could focus on my situation I suddenly saw Nick Rees' convoy – four black G63s with blacked-out windows – speeding down George Street towards the Fashion Week site. Traffic was slow but motorists were actually giving way to the vehicles; Sydneysiders love an ultra VIP almost as much as the PR industry does.

'He's on the way, he's on the way,' Lulu relayed back to Anya on her BlackBerry. 'ETA five minutes. Make sure you're in position and check that his Himalayan spring water is properly chilled.'

Nick was being taken through a special entrance that had been created this year for the celebrities who didn't want to be seen by the models or the press. The paps would of course see the convoy arrive, but thanks to our security detail only Marco, our tame paparazzo, was going to get close enough to get a shot for the international media – and Queen Bee was taking half the fee, thank you very much. Thankfully the gentlemanly Marco, with his button-down, crisp shirts and pressed jeans, always followed through on every deal. Most celebs loved him because he treated them with respect. Hell, he even treated me with respect, always tipping me off when other lensmen were planning to stitch us up. One thing I had learnt from working for Diane Wilderstein was to milk any opportunity for all it was worth, because you never knew when it would all end.

At least it was business as usual so far today. Marco would get a perfect set of pictures of Nick Rees and they would be up on the *Daily Mail* website less than an hour later, netting us all a tidy sum. A sum which was going to come in handy with Project B now well on his or her way. (Call me a romantic because I had chosen not to learn junior's sex before giving birth, but I def had two names ready: Louis if it is a boy and Fifi if it's a girl.) Either way this baby was going to cost bucketloads of money – including, for a start, the price of this expensive Allison Palmer gown (there would be no returning it now, even after a special designer hand-clean at Florida in Double Bay).

'We'll be there in ten minutes,' Lulu urgently briefed someone on the other end of her BlackBerry. This would be my twenty-three-year-old righthand woman's very first experience of a birth and all that went with it. Lulu's total baby experience to date had been attending a couple of baby showers; and, sitting next to me in the car, her eyes were as wide as saucers as if she was watching some kind of wild thriller, but from the couch. Meanwhile, I took stock of my physical condition – still no pain, just discomfort and a bit of a queasy feeling, but I was so hyped up from the show and my waters breaking, I couldn't get any sort of read from my body about what was really going on. And I always felt like this during Fashion Week, just not with the added drama.

A few minutes later, the car went down into the hospital's underground car park and pulled up in front of a set of lifts. A nurse was waiting for me with a wheelchair.

'I'm not getting into that,' I told Lulu. 'What am I, a cripple all of a sudden? I'm quite capable of walking into the hospital on my own. I mean, what if someone sees me? And where the hell is Michael – has he left for the airport yet?'

Blame all those hormones running rampant but I was now questioning what kind of boyfriend I had on my hands anyway. Who went on a business trip to China when their girlfriend was just a week out from having his baby? It doesn't matter that I had insisted he leave because there was a huge deal in the offing which would net him a cool million dollars. That wasn't the point. It was time he stepped up to the plate, and the plate he was stepping up to better be made by Hermès.

'He's flying back as we sp-speak.' Lulu's stutter had suddenly returned, no doubt brought on by the stress of Fashion Week and the realisation that the way I was carrying on she might have to become an assistant midwife right here in the car park. Well, I've always said that my Bees have to be versatile and adaptable.

Saintly, our driver, was all business. His real name is Stevie, but he'd earnt his nickname by getting us out of many pickles and also for the number of times he'd pulled an all-nighter as he waited to bring one of our clients back from Sydney's drinking site in the middle of the harbour, The Island, in the early hours of the morning. The celebrity who'd given him the most trouble was the pop-star daughter of a famous actress – she'd tried to get the happily married Saintly back to her hotel room. He'd been on the verge of banning all Queen Bee work after that, but we had managed to talk him round with a little help from Michael. Now he was almost part of the family. Saintly walked swiftly around to open the door to take me firmly by the arm, while signalling to the slightly startled nurse to bring over the wheelchair.

'Come on, Jasmine, take a load off,' he insisted, handing my prized Birkin bag to the trembling Lulu. I relinquished it but held on to my personal phone for dear life; Lulu was welcome to man the other three devices just while I got settled. I was beginning to feel an ache like the period from hell had just started. It felt putrid, and the thought of trying to deal with the nosy fash pack threatened to make me throw up more dramatically than Belle Single after a night on vodka shots.

Right then I forgot about any objections I'd had to the indignity of riding around in a wheelchair. In fact I've never been so thankful for a seat since that Emirates flight attendant introduced me to the many comforts and attributes of 1A.

So this was what it felt like to have a baby.

Ⴤ

Of all the sights on show at the Prince of Wales Private Hospital that afternoon, perhaps none quite matched the one that greeted staff when the lift doors finally opened on the delivery room floor. There I was in my shimmery Allison Palmer dress, now limp and ruined, a pair of Chanel shades all but welded to my eyes, and close behind was small blonde Lulu, white as a sheet, carrying my Birkin bag, her Céline Trapeze tote, several phones, and the all-important Fashion Week manifesto for day one.

'Oh my goodness, what do we have here, disco mum?' said a fifty-something nurse wearing a teddy bear badge with her name on it: Milly. She was evidently the maternity suite equivalent of Queen Bee's meeter and greeter, but right now I wasn't up for her droll humour. In fact, the way my insides felt as though they were being ripped apart, I didn't think I was up to very much at all.

'You can sit over there, dear,' Milly said to Lulu. Before I could point out that I needed my personal assistant with me at all times, Lulu plonked herself down on a comfy chair in the small reception area, a look of sweet relief on her face. It seemed Lulu wasn't quite ready to hear about the ins and outs of my birthing canal right at the moment; her plan was no doubt to greet Project B when he or she had been bathed and was preferably modelling an Adrienne & The Misses Bonney romper suit. No doubt in Lulu's mind, anything else was beyond the call of duty. Hell, the only way she had been able to stomach watching *Grey's Anatomy* was because she simply could not get enough of Drs McDreamy and McSteamy. After being processed, I was taken through to a small room and helped up onto a bed, where I received the first of what would be many examinations.

'The baby's at the starting blocks but they're not going to be diving in for a few hours yet,' Nurse Milly cheerfully announced from my business end. 'You're only two centimetres dilated. You have Dr CK Coach, right? Luckily we'll catch him before lunch – he doesn't like to be called after he's sat down unless baby is well and truly on its way.'

'Fine,' I managed, 'then will you please send in my assistant? We have work to do.'

'Well, good luck with that,' responded Milly, who obviously couldn't wait to head back to the nurses' station and tell them all about the bizarre first-time mum who thought she was in control. Once those contractions started in earnest, this trainee mama wouldn't be able to concentrate on anything – especially not work. It was what happened with many first-time mums – they were often in denial at just how massively their lives were changing. Having a baby was not exactly like having a mini-cosmetic procedure in your lunch break.

Lulu sheepishly entered the room in a tangle of mobile phone cords and files. 'Michael's def on his way back,' she reported. 'He was just boarding the plane when I called and he wants you to hang on for him. I was going to bring the phone in for you to talk to him but they said you needed some privacy.'

'What! I thought that he was already in the air?' I said, feeling testy.

'Nah, he was just on his way to the airport when we spoke the first time,' reported Lulu, looking even more nervous if that was possible. 'He's due to fly in first thing in the morning. It's a Cathay Pacific flight and I think it gets in just before six am.'

Fan-fucking-tastic. I had no plans in prolonging this birth until then. He could bloody well watch the video replay afterwards. In the meantime, I needed someone with a bit of influence around here to get me moved to a more luxurious suite away from Nurse Ratched as I had already christened Milly. After all, Michael's father, Bruce Lloyd, played golf with Dr Austin Smythe, some ancient specialist who was on the Prince of Wales Hospital board. But just when I was about to ask Lulu to try to get Michael's dad on the line so I could speak to him, she told me some really startling news.

The newest *The Voice* judge Ricky Martin had turned up unannounced at the Allison Palmer show with his adorable, four-year-old twins Valentino and Matteo (was it a sign that with Project B on the way, I better start looking at junior A-lists?). Apparently he did RSVP but that response must have been lost in translation somewhere. Of course, all three would have to be seated in the front row. This meant there had to be a radical rearrangement. But who to dump?

'Allison's family members?' Lulu asked hopefully, because she hated to have to be mean to any of her fashion pals.

'Are you kidding? That would be a very bad look,' I said. 'Take out any fashion assistants and leave only the fashion editors and directors. Okay ...'

'Bloggers?' tried the ever-hopeful Lulu, who never had to deal with bloggers – that was Angel's domain.

'No, they're the most important of all,' I reminded her. 'Most of them reach three times more people than the majority of the fashion mags. That's why they're known as "influencers".'

Ricky Martin's appearance had thrown us into chaos. But it wasn't his fault. Of course he had been invited to the show and the fact that he had brought his children along could result in a front-page picture right around the world. You couldn't buy that kind of publicity. We just had to ensure there would always be Allison Palmer signage in every frame that the paps got of him and the kids. It was just a darn shame that when it came to being prepared his RSVP had gone AWOL. We had just expected that like most stellar A-listers, he couldn't be bothered to respond at all.

'Lulu, we're just going to have to add three extra seats to the front row,' I said, knowing full well that it was already so squished that the person seated at the very end was almost backstage in the models' changing room – good thing that the junior Martins really were pintsized.

Suddenly it came to me in a rush of pregnancy hormones. Move that sarcastic gossip columnist Wally Grimes of *The Echo* and his fashionista mate Georgia Bunt, who writes very occasional pieces for the *International Tribune*, into Row B; then we only had to find one more seat. It really didn't matter about demoting Wally and Georgia, as they would only write sneering reports of the Allison Palmer show anyway – she was far too commercial for them. But Wally would now be especially furious at not sharing the front row with both Nick Rees and Ricky Martin. Too bad. Wally had written one cruel column too many about me in the past. And he had stopped just short of suggesting that I'd slept with Matt Ashley after the cricketer had all but attacked me.

'And Lulu,' I said, easing myself back on the pillows, which now felt delightfully soothing on my back, 'make sure they're shifted to the Siberian end of Row B. I don't want Wally putting one of his big, fleshy mitts on Nick's shoulder when he asks him for a quote – as for Ricky Martin, he is going to be hypersensitive to any unwelcoming pawing because he has his family with him. (Even if he didn't, the last thing that the hugely desirable Latino singer would want was to be pressured by a gossip columnist, especially one like Wally Grimes who didn't take no for an answer.)

No sooner had I got out my directive than my body was consumed by a contraction, which left me anxious about finding some pain relief.

'Epidural?' I asked Nurse Milly, who had bustled back in to keep an amused eye on proceedings.

'Not yet, dear,' she said briskly. 'You still have a way to go before you can get that sort of relief.'

I shot her a disbelieving stare, and turned back to Lulu to go over the next few hours again. Security had already been briefed about what should happen when the show ended, with a contingent of security guards ushering the super VIPs, including the editors of *Vogue* and *Harper's Bazaar*, backstage to a special room where Allison and several of her supermodels would be waiting, as well as interviews with vogue.com.au and a special Fashion Week photo essay for *Harper's*. What was not going to happen was that the no-name bloggers and fashion writers with a circulation of twenty thousand and under were going to monopolise anyone's time.

Thankfully, this might be the last Fashion Week to which I was going to have to pay such acute attention, since the Queen Bee agency was officially being acquired by Ivan Shavalik and his wife, Svetlana. The cashed-up Russians had officially made an offer that I couldn't refuse shortly after we had landed some pretty major accounts. Of course, I had knocked them back initially but, after feeling so miserable early on in the pregnancy, it had seemed like a fabulous idea. The money was fantastic and, while the deal included the naming rights to the agency, there was a juicy two-year contract for me as a consultant. Consulting was going to be my new It job, and my fees were as plump as Mel B before she hit Jenny Craig. It would hardly matter that I was also contractually prevented from starting another PR company for five years. That would take me right up to the time when Project B was about to start school. Perfect. Let someone else deal with all the crazies and their inflated ideas of their own worth – like Lidia Blue, who had invented gel chicken fillets to slot into the bra to make the wearer look like Kim Kardashian and who had wanted me to make her as famous as Steve Jobs for her services to the flat-chested. From now on I was going to keep most of the really annoying clients at a distance of not less than twenty kilometres as I got on with the serious business of being a mum. For the next five years at least, I would be taking an extended vacation to Disneyland as far as the fashion industry was concerned. My office was shifting to my home, and I was going to do something else really radical: I was going to start cooking regular meals, including breakfast. Right now we didn't even own a toaster – Michael thought our breakfast nook was table number five at Jackies in Paddington (the inside table with a panoramic view of the courtyard, so we would always know exactly who was coming). Yes, a brand-new life awaited us – all I had to do was sign on the dotted line.

Of course, the way I felt right now I couldn't have signed anything. I was in so much pain I couldn't even see the dotted line.

2

It wasn't how I'd pictured my birthing experience – not that I had been able to give it much thought, in between all those meetings and the craziness of my life in PR. But propped up on the bed and hooked up to all those monitors, which would register foetal distress if Project B was in trouble, was not how I imagined this new start to life would kick off. I even had some kind of drip feeding into the back of my hand, which made answering the phone a bit awkward, and still nothing had really got started yet. So far, giving birth was not exactly bone-shakingly life-affirming – it was just a series of progressively worse cramps.

Still, I didn't really understand what everyone had been on about when they spoke about the pain of childbirth. But then maybe I have a higher pain threshold than most people.

You've got to in this job. Otherwise how could I put up with people like Sydney's WAG du jour, Raelene Bax (the knitwear-designing fiancée of one of Australia's most famous international actors, Josh Sweetwood), and her manager, Sharon, who was one tough bitch, judging from the emails she sent through on Raelene's behalf, insisting that she had final approval on all photographs taken of her plus she got to keep all the clothes loaned to her for a shoot, as well as the jewellery? Sharon was a real ball-breaker. It was just a shame that we could never get her on the phone or schedule a meeting. It had taken us a couple of weeks to work out that the elusive Sharon didn't exist at all – she was just a figment of Raelene's imagination. It was a pity that this was also the extent of Raelene's creativity – especially when it came to giving dopey, uptight answers in interviews. ('Where's your favourite spot to holiday, Raelene?' 'Oh, I'm sorry but that's classified.') How thrilled was I going to be to put Raelene in my too hard and torturous basket for now.

'How are you, Jazzy?' Lulu came back into the room still looking terrified by what she might see. I noticed that she was carrying my Louis Vuitton Keepall, which had apparently just been dropped off by Saintly, who had picked it up from Maria, my housekeeper. The Keepall had been pre-packed by Lulu and me just last week after Lulu had got the idea from reading the final chapters of *What To Expect When You're Expecting*, no doubt trying very hard to avoid the gory bits. Lulu's job was to brief me about what the baby's birth and first days would be like, but on a strict need-to-know basis for both of us.

Before I could answer, three phones rang at once.

When there's a crisis in the office, all the phones go off at the same time, the incoming call lights flashing up almost as intensely as the New Year's Eve fireworks. So when the caller ID revealed Marshall Coutts' number on my mobile and on Lulu's handsets at the same time, I knew straight away that something big was going down. I felt it in my recently drained waters. Marshall was the senior partner in the law firm that handled all our business.

As she took the call and listened for a moment, Lulu's face went a disturbing shade of green (so not her colour). I could hear some key words in his excitable upper-class English accent: something about Ivan and cancelling the contract. Surely not?

I grabbed the phone from Lulu, who by now looked as if she was going to faint.

'Hello, Marshall. Yes, you do have me at a bad time,' I said in response to his query. I couldn't believe he was still going through the formalities of a mobile phone chat. 'Yes, I'm in the freakin' delivery suite and about to give birth.'

Marshall launched into an explanation. 'Well, just to let you know, we're tearing up all the contracts because Ivan doesn't have a business visa. In fact, he doesn't have the correct entry papers into Australia at all. How he managed to get into this country is a wonder – not to mention what exactly he's up to here. Looks like his acquiring of Queen Bee was all a front to make him look respectable. Indeed . . . Jasmine, I hate to be the bearer of bad news – particularly at such an, ahem, delicate time – but it appears that Ivan Shavalik could be a member of the Russian mafia We'll know more when our investigator's reports come through.'

Maybe they should patch Marshall's phone call into the rooms of all expectant mothers, because – whether it was the agitated tone of his voice or those alarming words – it seemed to do the trick as far as Project B was concerned. Right then, I felt the mother of all contractions. Either that or the lower half of my body had decided that it no longer wished to hang out with the top half. I couldn't help it, I let out a large, wild yelp similar to the sound that escapes from your lungs when you suddenly lose altitude on Magic Mountain.

'Arrrgh!' I dropped the phone, which was hastily retrieved by Lulu.

'Pardon! Pardon! Jasmine, are you there?' I could hear Marshall almost hyperventilating on the other end of the phone, but for once I couldn't deal with it because I now understood what everyone had been going on about when it came to giving birth.

If a nurse had not suddenly materialised by my side to give me some gas, I swear I would have got poor Lulu to push my bed into the nearest operating theatre. Hell, I was ready for a do-it-yourself caesarean just to relieve the pain.

Thankfully, the gas soon made me feel so blissed out that not even the clearly shady Ivan Von Shonkmeister was getting to me anymore, although I knew all too well what the news spelt out for me. After the birth, it was going to be back to the frenetic Queen Bee business as usual. My dream of having someone else make all the tough decisions, while I flitted in and out with marketing briefs, was not about to happen any time soon – unless Marshall had been massively wrong about the Russians.

Y

It turned out to be one of the longest nights I had ever experienced, punctuated by increasingly hideous contractions but without making much progress in actually giving birth. It was as if the kid had changed its mind about coming out for a meet and greet. Who knows, maybe he or she was in search of another exit and exhibiting an early streak of creativity.

Michael couldn't have timed his arrival better, although at first I thought I was hallucinating when he put his head around the door, all deep blue eyes and wavy brown hair which now framed his face instead of being slicked back in his regular businessman style. He looked adorable, although I would never dream of telling him that. We don't need to feed anyone's ego here.

'How are you both doing, Jazzy?' he asked softly, beaming at me, and I suddenly remembered that the reason I was feeling so trippy right now was because I was in the act of giving birth.

'She's only five centimetres dilated,' Nurse Ratched informed Michael as if I was not also present in the room. 'She's doing very well – she's being a very, very good girl.'

But Michael wasn't listening. He was fumbling with something that seemed to be stuck in his pocket.

'Jazzy Lou, will you marry me?' he said, finally pulling out a small red Cartier box and dropping down on one knee on Nurse Ratched's freshly swabbed floor. At least he wasn't going to catch anything: judging by the smell of it, the world's supply of antiseptic was contained between these walls.

I peered into the Cartier box, while Lulu worked hard at making herself invisible. Sitting on the cream silk was a huge diamond ring – when it came to picking the right stone, for the first time in his life, Michael had ordered that it be super-sized. This bauble was glinting so much in the harsh hospital lights that Project B better be born with a pair of sunnies on.

Funny, in the past I had been a bit anti-marriage. It was all a little bit suburban to me. I just didn't see myself in trackies pushing a trolley around a supermarket, filled with 'kitchen staples'. I mean, seriously, the thought of it almost gave me hives. So, despite the closeness of my relationship with Michael and the impending birth of our child, I hadn't allowed myself to dwell on this outcome. But now Michael had asked, I suddenly realised that this is what I had wanted all along. Or maybe I was simply delirious!

'Of course I will,' I said as I struggled to get the ring onto my lefthand finger which was already swollen with the extra baby fluid. Just then, another wrenching pain coursed through me and I flailed out, wildly reaching for the gas mask. 'Keep it for me,' I said in a muffled way through the mask, but I think he got the general idea.

The problem with having a society obstetrician is that they're always so busy socialising they don't have time for much else. The midwives' call to Dr CK Coach's phone was put through to his paging service, with the operator full of assurances the message would be passed on.

'Don't worry dear,' Nurse Ratched said reassuringly. 'I'm sure doctor will be along sooner or later. He hardly ever misses a birth.'

Michael's brows started to furrow dangerously. I sensed an explosion was imminent.

Only then did I remember that Dr CK Coach and his wife, Suzy, a former lifestyle writer for *Bizarre* magazine, had wanted to be invited to the Teak collection breakfast launch, which was being held at the back of the Opera House.

The Teak fashion show was run by one of my favourite Bees, Lauren, who was almost as offbeat as Teak's designers Bo and Lila, who were currently in their New Romantic revival period. But as well as looking the part, Lauren could handle any situation.

'Quick, Lulu, ring Lauren and tell her to get a message to Dr CK Coach that he needs to get his arse in a car right now and come to deliver this baby. I seem to recall that we seated the doctor and his guest at the very end of the front row just above the photographers' pit. This was where we put all the clients who insisted on being sat in the front row; it gave them a taste of all the hysteria of Fashion Week without interfering with the natural order of the magazine editors and different publishing companies, facing off across the runway. Everyone knew that if there was a Never Never Land section of the front row, above the photo pit was definitely where it was at.

The problem with dispensing instructions while giving birth was that everything seemed ten times more dramatic than it really was thanks to the bloodcurdling screams that kept involuntarily escaping from the side of the gas mask. In fact, Project B was now so determined to make his or her way into the world that I was starting to think my obstetrician might not even get here in time. He probably couldn't tear himself away from the Teak after-party at Bennelong.

Suddenly a clammy hand wiped the sweat off my forehead. Michael was trying to make himself useful but I had almost forgotten about him and our recent engagement. Even the dodgy Russians failed to get me going at the moment because it was already excitement central here, in a really bad way. So kill me now, I thought, as my body was racked by pain that not even a roomful of gas could help control. I needed an epidural – hell, I needed two epidurals, but the midwives were reluctant to administer one without my obstetrician, whom Lulu assured me was now on his way back from Fashion Week. Pity we didn't know any friendly cops who could give him a police escort.

Finally he burst into the room, brandishing Teak's program, with meticulous notes on it of the clothes that Suzy just had to have. (Personally, I thought she was a bit long in the tooth for rocking the Teak look, but this certainly wasn't the time or the place to bring that up now.)

'Absolutely fantastic show,' he said. 'Congratulations, Jasmine! Now, I'll just give this list to Lulu here for Suzy and then let's get on and have our baby, shall we?'

I moaned deeply in response – a sound that felt like it had escaped from somewhere deep inside me, which was currently having the workout from hell.

Michael, who had been threatening to do all sorts of things to Dr CK Coach for his slack attitude towards us during the past couple of hours, could hardly contain himself. 'You have to do something about this pain,' he insisted. Poor Michael – jetlag, a proposal and now he was trapped in the house of horrors where he was about to become a dad. (Lulu told me later that Michael looked so pale, she considered ordering him a blood transfusion – not that she wasn't a whiter shade of pale herself.)

'Quite right, and that's what we're going to do right now. Why don't you get a cup of tea while we assess the situation? Lulu, perhaps the two of you might care to visit the cafe together?' Dr CK Coach had explained to me that he was all for letting partners and significant others be there for the birth but felt that they just got in the way in the early stages.

A grateful Lulu almost ran out the door. She was ready to be there for me, but preferably from another suburb. I nodded for Michael to go and couldn't help noticing that he also seemed to be relieved to be heading for the door after Lulu, taking all the constantly flickering mobile phones with them. Well, almost all – I had the bat phone secreted under the covers because, even in this extreme pain, I still wanted to find out what was going on with the Russians and whether this meant that the deal was definitely off. In fact, I was starting to wonder whether it had really happened. I was high as a model at an after show party on all that gas – had I just imagined Marshall's phone call?

The doc was having a hard time examining me because I was in so much pain I couldn't stay long in one position. But the slight twitch in his brow told me that despite his impeccable bedside manner he was concerned about something to do with my baby. I kept hearing the word caesarean being mentioned, and before I knew it I was being prepped for an operation, and Michael was in the room again, even more ashen-faced. A screen was put up around me at the business end of proceedings. As the pain blocks started to kick in and Michael took my hand, the last thing I was aware of was the mobile phone blinking rapidly. The messages were already coming in thick and fast.

3

A strange but oddly familiar tune punctuated my dreams and for several moments I had no idea where I was or what had just taken place, seemingly another lifetime ago. A quick glance at the beautiful baby asleep in the crib beside the bed confirmed that we had both survived the eleventh-hour caesarean, although Michael, now slumped in the chair, had not fared as well, briefly passing out before Fifi was born.

Yes, a baby daughter, born right in the middle of Fashion Week, and she already had pretty pink rosebud lips. We had both decided that if it was a girl, she would be called Frances after Michael's much loved grandmother, who had recently passed away. But I had already made him promise that if it was a girl she would be called Fifi for short. Frances was just her formal name if she wanted to be prime minister or run a major corporation. Of course, she could do that I thought, looking at her again proudly. I now felt full of the wonder of the world. Who would have thought that I had just given birth and yet all the pain seemed to have faded away. I certainly didn't want whatever they had given me to wear off any time soon. But what was that sound? Ah yes, the bat phone. I picked it up just as I heard the flurry of footsteps outside in the hallway.

'Yes?' I said groggily.

'Jazzy? How ARE you?'

Only one person sounded so Aussiewood: Ciara, Queen Bee's first and probably last management contract, judging by how full-on she was about making us earn our percentage of the earnings we signed her up to.

'Um, I've just given birth,' I responded, listening to my own voice and wondering whether I sounded more maternal all of a sudden — or was it just those painkillers kicking in which added another layer of huskiness?

'Congrats, go you. What did you have?' she cooed insincerely, not waiting for an answer before plunging on. 'Jazzy, remember I'm doing that Fashion Week bronzer launch today? Can I Skype you my outfit? I'm not really sure it's working.'

Ciara sounded petulant, and I almost didn't have the heart to tell her that the last thing I planned to do in these precious hours (had it only been an hour?) after giving birth was act as her stylist. Not for the first time did I curse myself for giving Ciara access to my most private of numbers. But who would have thought that such a sex goddess as her could be so needy?

I went on, 'You know, I thought we'd decided that you would wear the hot-pink Trelise Cooper sequined shift, sweets. My Skype has been playing up all morning here,' I lied, 'but I'm going to send Anya straight over to help you get dressed, okay?'

'No, Jazzy, you're IT when it comes to choosing my wardrobe.'

'Sorry, what?' I said weakly. 'I can't hear you. I think there must be something wrong with this line.' And with that I hung up. Ciara could find someone else to torture.

For the next ten minutes, I stared at Fifi, who was definitely the most beautiful baby I had ever seen and who appeared to be sleeping soundly, I was pleased to see.

From the corner of my eye I noticed that Michael had started to stir, and I tried to remember whether I had told him that the Russian deal had fallen through so it would be back to work as usual. He wasn't going to like that. I had better get that stunning ring onto my finger quick smart before he changed his mind about the whole engagement thing.

Thank goodness for jet lag, because Michael had just gone straight back to sleep again. I wanted to do that too, because those painkillers they had given me had def done the job, but now they were knocking me sideways. I should have been organising Anya to look after Ciara, but each time I tried to rouse myself to call her I found that I had drifted off again. Celebrity management really was a bigger headache than working in public relations as it involved huge egos and major insecurity. Nowhere in Ciara's management contract was there a clause stating that her management arm had become her newly minted slaves overnight, but it would now be up to Anya to dress Ciara, update her tweets, organise her hair and makeup appointments, and blow her nose if she needed that done as well.

'Are we awake yet, dear?'

Yet another of the nurses had arrived in my room and seemed intent on getting me up, which made no sense to me at all. Apparently it was important for me to try to use the toilet. Great, my bottom half felt so tender that I would have been quite happy if someone had given me diapers – if they were good enough for astronauts, they were fine by me. It was only once I was settled back in bed again, gazing down adoringly at Fifi in her crib with a happy but bleary-eyed Michael by my side, that I remembered I had to give permission for Marshall Coutts to phone Ivan the Terrible to call off the deal. But how to break it to him without causing shocking repercussions? I could be on the receiving end of a poisoned umbrella tip in the leg, or perhaps a toxic Russian Mule? And now that the deal was off, how would I manage going back to work straight away with a baby at home? In fact, how would I manage anything? Just the thought of standing up again seemed like an impossible feat right now, up there with running a marathon.

In spite of my worries, I smiled again to see Fifi sleeping so peacefully in her crib. The kid didn't seem to be the type to wake up and demand a feed every half hour. This would bode well for her in the future, if she ever wanted to attempt a diet.

I was just about to slip back to sleep, thanks again to the painkillers – how sweet they were, just the thing to help me deal with several of Queen Bee's more demanding clients. As I drifted off, I thought about François Gitame, the celebrity chef we'd foolishly taken on believing that he could cook for our very important clients and we could cross-promote at major events. But it hadn't worked out that way. François was so full on that he required a Bee in the kitchen with him when he was cooking at high-profile events. The minder's job was to photograph each one of his special dishes and then send the shots directly to the media for inclusion in the following day's paper. Like yeah, 'Hold the front page – a picture of François's prawn taco coming down the line.' He also thought we should do a news story about the witty way he had deconstructed the humble hamburger. What, did he think the mighty *Sun* newspaper had become the *Hamburger News?*

The insistent buzzing of a phone within my dream slowly brought me back to the hospital room. The phone, lying on the bed just out of my grasp, was going off. I reached for it with an effort.

Maude, ringing from the office, sounded jumpy, even for her. 'Jazzy – so fabulous to hear about Fifi's birth,' she said hastily, 'but a van has arrived at the office filled with furniture and they want everything out, even your desk, and I don't know what to tell them.' Her voice trailed off with a little whimper and I heard Anya take control of the situation. She had evidently taken the receiver right out of Maude's shaky paws.

'Don't worry about it, Jazzy Lou,' she declared. 'You need to rest. I'll just tell them to come back tomorrow once we have proper instructions. It's just Ivan Shavalik trying to get ahead of himself by moving his stuff in, but it's a little too early for that, isn't it?'

It sure was. It looked like Ivan and Svetlana were not going to take the news that they were in deep shit with the Department of Immigration on the chin. Of course, they were going to appeal and in the meantime were clearly trying to set themselves up in 'Bee-land'. Thank goodness for Anya.

Sure enough, the next moment I could hear her laying down the law to whoever had turned up. 'No, I don't know what you're supposed to do with the van,' she said, sounding exasperated. 'And I can't see how it's really my problem. Don't come back until someone rings your boss, okay?'

With not a moment to spare and Fifi starting to stir in her crib, I quickly hung up and rang Marshall Coutts' mobile, giving him the rundown on what was going on.

'Are you sure they won't be able to do business here?' I asked, sounding as groggy as my BFF Luke, after one of his monumental benders.

'Absolutely Jasmine,' he responded. 'Believe me, you do not want to be around when this all goes wrong. It's the sort of association that will lose all credibility for you.'

I'd certainly spent too many long hours working on my brand to lose it like that. We should really have investigated the Russians before we started negotiations, but the thought of that major payout and then working as a highly paid consultant had made me lose track of basic businesses procedures. I had just been too greedy.

'Okay,' I agreed. 'Tear up those contracts now. Do whatever you have to do and offer them money for their moving bills – they've already had someone bringing furniture to the office.'

'That's ridiculous,' Marshall exploded over the phone. 'You're not responsible for anything – the contract hasn't been signed and legalled.'

'Look, I understand that,' I told him, 'but the last thing I need is some pissed-off Russians on my doorstep. It's bad enough that we're not going ahead with the deal.'

Later, once I had finished feeding Fifi and an exhausted Michael had gone home to sleep in our own bed, I started to formulate a plan that would get rid of the Russians for good and allow me to keep Queen Bee in safe hands. I would try to get them to buy into Diane Wilderstein's agency while they tussled with the Australian authorities. She was desperate enough to sacrifice her reputation in order to be flush with Russian funds. I would find a way to make this work. It was genius.

There were zillions of accounts out there that they could go after together and it would get Diane off my back when it came to trying to upstage my events. She would be so busy getting everything set up with Ivan and Svetlana that she would scarcely have time to come up for air.

But how to get them together? With Marshall's help I would pen a letter to Ivan and Svetlana, thanking them for their interest in Queen Bee but informing them that Fifi's birth had made me want to retain my own agency. However I would be happy to recommend Wilderstein PR as the most suitable agency for them because Diane Wilderstein is one of the most respected PRs in the industry and had actually taught me everything I know.

4

Checking out of the Prince of Wales Private was the first thing on my mind, but seemed to be the last thing on everyone else's. Nurse Ratched and all her underlings, the 'Ratcheds', seemed determined to keep Fifi and me there as long as possible. We were to be hostages to lousy food, ridiculous visiting hours and a smell of antiseptic that no amount of Agent Provocateur or monster bouquets from Mr Cook and Grandiflora could overpower.

The one saving grace was that Michael had been busy bringing me my favourite meals from Jackies (breakfast), Bills (lunch) and Azuma restaurant (dinner). I sound spoilt but when you work the hours I do, cooking is the lowest thing on your priority list. Besides, I regard eating out as a legitimate expense because I meet so many contacts that way and I can see what all of them are wearing. You can't be in fashion PR and not pay attention to what's being worn in some of the hottest destinations in Sydney. So it wasn't as if I was going to sacrifice my A-list diet while being stuck in hospital. I had just given birth to a beautiful daughter. I wasn't supposed to be doing penance.

Admittedly, I was still very sore and on painkillers but surely it was better to make a move now than to be treated like an invalid here? Besides, I could always call some kind of home nursing service and get all the help I needed, plus there was Anna, our fabulous nanny who had been in the family for years. Fifi would have nurses on site 24/7. Most importantly, our home would be a much more secure base to deflect any sudden visitors speaking with a Russian accent. I was already concerned about waking from a sleep and seeing Ivan and Svetlana standing next to my bed at visiting time.

'You'll be with us here for another two days at least, until you start to heal from the surgery,' Nurse Ratched informed me.

I started to wonder whether she was bribable. Would a famous Queen Bee goodie bag do the trick? Or perhaps I could get her a couple of tickets to Beyoncé's next concert, or slip her a wad of fifty-dollar bills? If that didn't work I told myself we would walk anyway, although even I could see that in my current state, making a fast getaway with Fifi would be tricky. Hell, I almost needed Noah, my Israeli personal trainer, to set up camp at my place just to help me out of bed and to the bathroom so I could take what had become some of the most uncomfortable pees of my life. It would certainly be a long time before that 'end of town' was back to normal, and the thought of trying to have sex again was something I was prepared to postpone till this time next year. I'm sure Michael and I would have learnt about the after-effects of a caesarean during the birth classes – if only we'd been able to schedule one in.

I checked my Rolex, which I found in the top drawer of the table next to my bed. It read twelve o'clock but for a moment I didn't know whether it was midday or midnight.

Now the light was flashing on my mobile phone again. The number on the screen lit up in front of my eyes but it was meaningless to me in my current state. This having-a-baby thing was definitely worse than jet lag. That's another thing they don't tell you about. Or maybe they would have . . .

'Yes,' I said weakly as I picked it up. 'Queen Bee.' What the hell was I thinking answering the phone in this state? I had officially lost it!

Rochelle Crawford, the fashion editor of *Bizarre*, must be the only fashionista in town not to have caught up on the fact that my waters had broken just before Allison's show. Rochelle is so self-obsessed that she is officially beyond gossip, except when it directly involves her or her competition. So it was not at all surprising she would ring now to complain that her assistant was seated two rows back in Trelise Cooper's show. Oh, the indignity of it all – the queen of the fashionistas must have her entourage around her at all times.

'Jazzy, remember I sent you an email about this last week,' she shouted down the phone.

'Rochelle, I'm a little, um, indisposed right now, but Lulu is right on it,' I assured her, trying to sound both conciliatory and efficient. And with that I hung up and sank back on my pillows. If the worst thing that happened at Fashion Week was that Rochelle Crawford was unhappy with the placement of her assistant, then it was a stellar success. Let her swelter in Row C, I thought, glancing at my watch; Trelise's show was about to start and then it really wouldn't matter at all because Rochelle would be concerned about the next possible slight from a designer at the other big show of the day. What's more, something told me that if Rochelle was going to be that petty, she could be on shaky ground. Fashion editors were officially an endangered species at the moment because there were so many innovative bloggers coming along. And Rochelle Crawford should have received the memo others had, including a couple of blogger superstars.

All morning the flowers had been arriving, because when you're the PR queen of Sydney and you've just had a baby they're more or less a given. But even I was blown away when two hundred pale pink Brazilian roses were delivered to my room by three giggling nurses.

'Congratulations, you've just made Prince of Wales Private history,' said the cheeriest nurse, whose curly ginger hair made her look a little like a cherub. Huffing and puffing with the weight of my bouquet on steroids, they put it down on the floor in the corner because none of the hospital-issue furniture was strong enough to support that weight.

But who could they be from? Sure, Queen Bee had a lot of wealthy clients, but none who would wish to throw their money around like that. I thought of all the celebs I'd done favours for lately, including a certain US actor I'd introduced to a lesser-known star here. But surely they hadn't hit it off that well?

The podgy nurse passed me the card from the bouquet. *Congratulations on the birth of your daughter. We look forward to a long and fruitful future with you both. Ivan and Svetlana.* It was from the Russians. I should have guessed.

Great, clearly they hadn't got the bloody email from Marshall Coutts telling them the deal was off, plus my personal note recommending the dreaded Diane. But of course they were well aware, they were just refusing to accept it. This was about to get trickier than naming the winner for the *Coco Man of the Year Awards* when you had so many 'worthy' entrants.

I hit the buzzer next to my bed with all the gusto of a competitor on *Sale of the Century*. Almost immediately, Charna, my favourite nurse, stuck her head around the door. 'Everything okay, Mum?' she asked brightly. (I hated the way all the staff addressed the women as 'Mum' once they had delivered their babies. It was patronising.)

'Why don't you take these flowers and share them with the other mothers?' I said. 'You could get several decent bunches out of this.'

'Really, are you sure?' she said, attempting to pick up the hefty container before I changed my mind. 'Everyone would love them.'

'Absolutely,' I replied. 'I have more than enough.' Quite frankly, that mega bunch of roses was not only making me nervous but the fragrance was almost suffocating me. It was a symbol of how I had royally screwed up my life. 'Just bring me back the pot, okay?' It was a French antique from Parterre in Woollahra. I didn't have to get up close to recognise it because I'd had my eye on it for ages – not that the Russians would have known that, unless they could read my thoughts.

The next call I made was to Marshall again, telling him about the flowers and asking him to send another letter to the Russians stating the current position.

'Absolutely Jasmine,' he responded. 'I'm afraid that it looks increasingly as though your friends Ivan and Svetlana did make a false declaration on their visa applications and they are currently being investigated for money laundering.'

OMG! This was getting ridiculous. The sooner I could get the Russians to hook up with Diane Wilderstein the better off I would be – although they were starting to look a bit shady even for her. But in the meantime, I definitely had to get out of this hospital and into the safety and security of my own home. And maybe it would be an excellent time to change all the locks.

𝚈

As Nurse Ratched had threatened, it took another two days before we were able to leave the hospital. This despite the fact that Anna was ready and waiting to look after Fifi, plus Charna was also going to be there when she wasn't rostered on at the hospital, which would give Anna some valuable time out. Charna was happy to help me out for the extra money but asked me to keep the arrangement top secret. The nurses weren't supposed to freelance but to keep their relationships with all new mothers inside the walls of the hospital. It was regarded as a conflict of interest if they all started running off with every neurotic new mum who needed them. Meanwhile, Queen Bee had been under siege. When word got out that I was out of action, every opportunist in town came to visit our office in Alexandria to try to get as much stuff as possible without me there watching them like a hawk.

The worst offender was the ageing stylist Jamie Moore. Jamie had unfortunately done one line of coke too many during his time in the fashion industry, and his behaviour was growing increasingly bizarre. He was now more famous as a serial freeloader who seldom returned the clothes than he'd once been as one of the city's hottest stylists. This was the sad downside of the fashion industry – the stylists who thought they were still relevant despite the fact that the industry had quickly moved on. These days, when you had eighteen-year-old bloggers being flown around the world for fashion shows, it mattered even less what magazine stylists on the fashion periphery decreed was cool. Jamie Moore was as 'current' as last year's obsession with jeggings. Meanwhile many of the fringe titles with limited circulation and resources were seriously out of date before they even hit the stands, and the platoons of fashion journalists who had once been feted had been totally upstaged by young kids with an entirely different and much more accessible agenda. The fashion hierarchy was rapidly being dismantled, and the beauty of the Queen Bee agency is that we were across it all, especially with our newly set-up talent arm to hook up the bloggeratti with some serious commercial deals.

Lulu called shortly after I arrived home from hospital informing me that Jamie, clad in a Miss Jay beret, a fake Burberry trench and toting a 'Birkin' fresh from the streets of downtown Bangkok, seemed ready to mount his version of a smash-and-grab raid on the Queen Bee showroom. (You ask how Lulu knew he was wearing cheap Asian copies of the fashion classics and that his career hadn't suddenly come good again? This was one of the first lessons my Bees learnt when they came to work for me and made the fatal mistake of bringing in a fake designer item to impress their workmates. We could smell it a mile off: the shade of leather was never quite right, the zippers were wobbly as hell and items of clothing just didn't sit right.)

'What do you want me to tell him?' Lulu whispered into the receiver. 'He says he's shooting for Hush magazine.'

Trust Jamie to pick a publication that only comes out a few times a year — by then he presumably hoped we would have forgotten all about his supposed shoot. Should we give him the benefit of the doubt, especially with Hush's fashion editor currently in London? Lulu couldn't exactly ring around to check while he was still on the premises: it would be too obvious. Jamie was going to be ultra pissed off if he really was working for Hush. Besides, everyone deserves a second chance. Even a has-been like Jamie Moore.

'Okay, let him at it,' I instructed Lulu. 'But watch him closely on the monitor and make sure you run an inventory of everything he's taken. Call me after he leaves and let me know how it went.' Well, that would be the Bees' morning's entertainment taken care of. With the closed-circuit TV trained on every area of the showroom, it would be easy to see what Jamie was up to when he was given free rein among the racks. That was how we had caught many a klepto in the past.

The phone rang again less than five minutes later. It seemed Jamie had reverted to his bad old ways. 'No sooner was he shown to the racks when he stashed a six-pack of Omni sparkling wine in his bag,' said a breathless Lulu. 'We were going to let him keep it – after all, it's hardly Cristal, is it? – but then he went for the Benefit makeup kits and the one-off Oliver Peoples collection that's supposed to be shot next week. We went in there and caught him red-handed. At first he pretended it was all for the shoot, but we kept questioning him. Finally he dropped everything except the Omni bubbles and we put him in a cab, clutching a twenty-dollar note in his hand.'

Thank goodness for Lulu, who was one of Queen Bee's most valuable assets. Leaving her in charge was definitely a gift from above. But with the action heating up faster than a Sydney summer, I knew that I would have to get back to work again really soon.

5

As it seemed the Russians wouldn't take no for an answer, insisting to Marshall of all people that there was an agreement set in place, there was only one way to get the message through to them. We had to make it very public.

I penned a strongly worded press release:

Queen Bee No Longer Up For Sale

One of Sydney's biggest fashion public relations agencies, Queen Bee, is to stay in local hands following a well-thought-out decision by founder and owner Jasmine Lewis not to sell to Russian interests.

'There has never been a more exciting but challenging time to be working in public relations,' said Lewis. 'I could not give it all up.

'Just as the media landscape has changed so rapidly, the role of the brand publicist has become increasingly important to ensure that the client's message is sent out to all the different forms of media, from established newspapers, magazines, television and radio stations to the most remote fashion blogger.'

Lewis, who recently gave birth to her first child, commented that she was loath to hand over to others the business she had started from scratch.

'I owe it to my staff of thirty and our high-profile clients to be here for them and take on the challenges side by side.'

If our Russian friends were under the misapprehension that the deal was still going through, this should make it abundantly clear to them. We sent the press release out to the trade press and to the media pages of most publications, plus the media websites and the advertising and marketing pages of the major newspapers.

Behind the scenes I also had my insider in the offices of *Eve Pascal* magazine talk loudly on the phone about how the Shavaliks were looking to buy into another agency now and it looked like they had Wilderstein PR in their sights.

My insider, codenamed Prada princess, sat right outside the wild-maned editor Lillian Richard's office – and Lillian was none other than one of Diane Wilderstein's confidantes. Once she heard that intel, Diane would be on the phone to Ivan faster than you could say 'blini with the lot'. Barely had

I pressed send when my phone rang with another potential disaster, although on a much smaller scale.

The frantic call came through from Anya, who was running a fashion show for the Meek & Mild label at Catalina restaurant.

'I'm so, so sorry to bother you,' she spluttered in that agitated way she had when everything was turning to shit. 'It's just that DJ M is missing in action from the set-up tonight, and when I called him he sounded quite sozzled. He put the phone down but forgot to hang up properly, and then I think he must have fallen asleep because all I could hear was him snoring.'

'Have you tried to find a stand-in?' I barked, waking Fifi. I couldn't help raising my voice: I just couldn't believe how my life had started to unravel – first there was a bunch of Russians less than thrilled with me for reneging on their suss deal to buy me out, and now a no-brainer client event had become a potential PR catastrophe. 'How about Garnet Gold?' Real name Deborah Planks: the celebutante and former media darling was always talking up her skills as a DJ. She would probably hold us to ransom on the price but at least she had some sort of 'cred'.

'We tried to call her already,' said Anya, 'but she's promoting some product over in Fiji. I think it's an energy drink or something.'

Of course she is, I thought – trust Garnet Gold to try to get in on the act of flogging Coconut Crunch – a product that Belle Single had tried unsuccessfully to push. Belle's main problem was that she took on far too many product endorsements, so she was no longer believable, Michael's-ex would even plug steak knives if she thought there was a bit of coin in it.

It was funny because, on a TV panel show, Garnet had paid Belle out big time for being so commercial and doing such a cheesy ad as the one for Coconut Crunch. Now here she was running around Fiji posing next to the coconut palms herself. Fabulous!

The concept for tonight's event was that DJ M would create just the right kind of chilled space for Meek & Mild's fashion installation featuring live models, and the guests could wander around and get a three-hundred-and-sixty-degree view of the clothes. Jayson Brunsdon had done it at Fashion Week the year before; everyone had loved it because it was such a welcome relief not to sit through yet another fashion show in the tight schedule.

'Anyway, Thelma has found a spare pair of headphones and she's going to give it a try,' said Anya.

Dear Thelma. At twenty she really looked the part with long hair balayaged to within an inch of its life, thanks to her pal, Amy, who was a junior at La Boutique and was always getting her in for training nights. She was even more hip-looking than Sass & Bide accessories diva, Chip Edwards. Thelma was definitely the most tuned in of the Bees, and if anyone could pull off being a hip DJ it was definitely her.

'Oh, and the other thing you should know is that I've just had a call to say that *The Voice* finalists will be turning up to the event,' Anya added, no doubt blushing almost as deep as her scarlet cropped top-do (she'd obviously tagged along to staff training at La Boutique too).

Okay, so no pressure – much! The hottest reality stars in Planet Sydney at the moment and at the turntables would be – ta da! – Thelma from Queen Bee doing her own 'audition' for *So You Want To Be A DJ?*

Why hadn't I chosen a less interesting but much more stable career in accounting, or maybe even real estate? Hell, maybe it wasn't too late to return to florist school. Anything but put up with this kind of insanity day and night.

I hadn't been planning to attend any parties for at least three months, and not until I had Fifi settled on the right feeding program. (Breastfeeding was not an option for me – I had ruled it out even before Fifi was born because it had never appealed to me. Life is all about knowing your own limitations – so we were all about trying different formulas until we found the one that suited Fifi best and had her contented enough to fall asleep. Right now a special organic version from Wholefoods House in Woollahra was doing the trick.) But I decided on the spot that I had to see Thelma DJ and make sure everything was running smoothly. With the press release having just gone out about not selling the agency to the Russians, it was a good opportunity to remind everyone that I was still in control.

But what to wear with my figure looking downright lumpy? I was still too sore from the emergency caesar to be able to return to my personal training program with Noah, who had simply prescribed light walking in an attempt to get me back in shape. Fortunately, I was usually too busy to get dressed up for Queen Bee parties, plus I had learnt early on the fatal mistake of tottering around in a pair of punishing Givenchy heels and a constricting frock when I was essentially there to work and often had to move fast on my feet. As a result, no one would expect a yummy red carpet mummy. In the end I put on my Céline tee, a Bassike skirt and high-top Marant trainers – the perfect look for slipping in and out of most venues without attracting a lot of attention.

I saw Meek & Mild's name in lights as soon as the car rounded the bend into Rose Bay. The pink and green laser display reflected on the harbour around the A-list restaurant, and from the moment I left the car at the valet park near the entrance, I could hear the sounds.

'Oh my God, Thelma, you're totally doing it,' said Violet, one of the newest of the Bees, standing close to the deck and rocking her tiny frame back and forth on enormous platform heels.

Well, at least there was one satisfied customer, but even I had to admit that Thelma sounded good – no doubt helped along by the excellent sound system.

Anya spotted me immediately, but I held up a finger to shush her as I wasn't ready to be the centre of attention and to show them all the photos of Fifi on my iPhone. I just wanted to ensure that everything was going well and that the lovely team behind Meek & Mild (who I knew had just flown in from New Zealand the night before) were happy, then I wanted to get back in my car and head home. If Fifi was sleeping when I got back I might even have some down time to work out a new plan for the agency. Calling off the Russian buyout was one thing, but actively taking the reins back was something else again. It would def have to be a case of 'Hold on, it's going to be a bumpy ride.' However, it seemed Anya had other plans for me. She hurried to my side and explained that Nicole Richie had just popped in with *The Voice* finalists and was being monopolised by the tiresome Wally Grimes. Meanwhile I could see my preferred gossip columnist and pal, Luke Jefferson, discreetly idling at a safe distance, waiting for Grimes to finish up. I could see that the reliably parched Luke was hell bent on getting his story, because he was clutching a cocktail but just as a prop. He had no intention of even taking a sip until he had some live quotes from Nicole all wrapped up.

When he spotted me, I winked at him and nodded in the direction of Wally so he would know that the situ was in hand. Then I turned to poor Anya with a very sweet public smile in case anyone clocked us and hissed at her, 'So Nicole bloody Richie! Why didn't anyone tell me? You said that some of *The Voice* finalists were coming along. Couldn't you have mentioned that the delicious, fashionista wife of one of the judges would be arriving as well? When it came to international style icons, Richie was right up there with Anna Wintour. And who let Wally Grimes near her?'

Anya tried to explain herself, saying that the first anyone knew of it was when tiny Nicole Richie slipped in, but I wasn't really listening to her.

'Also, isn't it a bit ambitious for Thelma to be DJing in front of Nicole? Anya, you have to ask her if she wants to slip on the headphones herself to play us some of her favourite sounds.'

But none of this was as important as extricating Nicole Richie from Wally Grimes, and I knew that I was the only woman for the job because the Network publicists who had accompanied her to the restaurant did not seem to be making much progress in moving her on. Wally was in full flight, his big fleshy lips with just a few crumbs of a particularly delicious canape clinging for dear life onto the corners of them.

'You're so tiny,' I heard him bleat. 'You probably haven't tried many restaurants here because you seldom eat at all, do you?'

I marched right up to the group but Wally well and truly saw me coming. 'Jazzy Lou, how lovely to see you. But shouldn't you be in a maternity wing somewhere giving birth?' he snarled, then purposefully turned his back to me.

A startled Nicole glanced at my tummy, and then quickly looked away not meaning to be rude. Okay, I def was nowhere near as slim as she was, but that tummy of mine, although a bit lumpy in places, wasn't that bad. You could tell I wasn't about to give birth.

'Nicole,' I said warmly, pointedly ignoring Wally now too. 'It's so great to have you here. Please do let me show you around.'

'Wait just a moment, Jasmine. I'm interviewing Nicole.' Wally looked fit to explode.

'Of course, you are,' I said over my shoulder. 'We'll be right back.'

And taking her tiny birdlike arm, the two of us sauntered off with the publicists and a relieved Luke Jefferson cautiously bringing up the rear. Wally accepted another glass of champagne from the waiter and went off to find some buddies, no doubt to complain about what a bitch I am. The problem for Wally was that his buddies were an endangered species. The way he kept selling out his friends, he had very few left.

There had been no roped off VIP section at Catalina when I had arrived, but there certainly was one there now thanks to Anya (who never left home without several metres of golden tassels in the back of her car). Catalina's owner, Michael McMahon, was happy to assist her to set it up, and SIPs (self important pests) like Wally Grimes were definitely not welcome.

'Get me that creep's number,' I hissed at Anya. (Wally Grimes was not someone I kept in my phone directory, let alone on speed dial, because even though he was a well-known columnist, he could never be trusted to put information to the best use, so what was the point?)

Anya quickly dialled the number for me and we both watched as he fumbled in his pocket for his phone. Fortunately, he never ignored a call, just in case one of his favourite contacts phoned to give him a juicy story. This was one man who could never afford to be out of mobile range.

'Ye-es,' he answered tentatively, while Richie started to talk to Luke Jefferson, who loved to hang out in LA and was now talking shops on Robertson with her.

'Wally!' I said through clenched teeth. 'Nicole won't be speaking to you again and if you attempt to bother her, this will be viewed as harassment.'

'Oh really?' he trilled. 'Well, don't expect me ever to write up one of your crummy events again.' He hung up the phone first, then we all watched as he flicked it onto the video setting and started filming himself talking into the camera. Now he was walking over to the roped off area and filming Nicole before a security guard came to him and tapped him on the shoulder.

'Mate,' he said. 'It's time to leave.' Then we all watched as Wally was moved away, pausing only to scoff another couple of canapes and drain his glass of bubbles, as he was escorted to the door.

In the following day's issue of *The Echo*, Wally wrote a bitchy piece about the evening, referring to our client as 'a tacky chain store label', and intimating that Nicole Richie had wanted to be in a special area because the smell of food was clearly making her ill. This was totally a lie – Nicole Richie had been a real sweetheart to deal with and everyone had raved about how lovely she was.

The Voice must really be slipping in the ratings, it read, *because on Wednesday night, they sent out the heavy artillery in the reed thin form of Nicole Richie, superstar wife of The Voice judge, Joel Madden, to the launch of a high street clothing label at Catalina.*

Clearly showing disdain for the clothing line, Richie declined to comment on the label or indeed anything much at all. Herded into a

VIP area by a platoon of minders, she looked particularly uncomfortable when the canapes came out. The poor dear clearly hasn't eaten a square meal in decades. (This was also BS – Nicole loved the canapes there so much, she quietly asked for a booking the following day to bring the family with her. And, as for the label, she wanted to debut it in LA, which just shows you that you certainly can't believe everything you read.)

He also said that she had refused an interview with the press, which wasn't correct because Luke Jefferson's piece, also published the next day but in *The Sun* (with a much higher circulation), had lots of great insights on how Nicole Richie, her husband, Joel Madden, and their children were enjoying their life in Sydney.

Bliss. The flowers that I sent as a thank you on behalf of the client to Luke's office were a talking point among his colleagues all week.

'They were totes fab,' Luke said over the phone. 'But next time you decide to send me the edited highlights of the Chelsea Flower Show, how about a ticket so I can see the real thing for myself.'

Heavens knows my old buddy deserved one.

6

Returning to the office just four days after giving birth to Fifi wasn't as bad as I thought it would be, but then everything after the immense effort of having a baby was going to be an anti-climax, like going to see Pink and leaving after the support act. Of course, it wasn't how I had expected early motherhood to go. I thought we'd be at home watching *The Ellen DeGeneres Show* on the couch as I lulled my newborn off to sleep. And if Fifi took after her mother at all, she would be asleep by the time Ellen's second guest had appeared and the audience were up to their sixth dance move. Truly nothing made me more drowsy than watching television − not even great sex. It was the leisure moment when all the energy I had expended throughout the day came crashing down and, before I knew what was happening, I was fast asleep on the couch. But there had been no time for that with all the Russian drama. First, Ivan had been calling me to try to assure me that whatever troubles he was experiencing with Immigration were just temporary, and he was in the process of appealing any restrictions. Then Svetlana phoned me wanting to meet for lunch so she could give me the latest collection of Baby Dior that she had purchased for Fifi. I had tried to explain that the birthing experience had suddenly made me determined to run my own agency, but they were having none of it. Finally, Ivan had shown his true colours and threatened me with breach of contract, although technically no contract had been signed. Outlined in a letter from his old-school establishment Sydney lawyers, Boyd, Boyd and Macarthur, was a hefty list of damages that included the cost of hiring an interior designer to refit the offices, furniture, removal costs and damages to his professional reputation, etc etc. However, as Marshall Coutts put it, Ivan's reputation was well dodgy to start with, and so it could be argued that it was hardly able to be further damaged.

Disappointingly, despite the fact that we were being billed for all the expensive French antique furniture, Marshall said that we would not be able to keep it as we would be fighting the claims all the way.

What exactly had I got myself into by having anything to do with the Shavaliks in the first place? I should have remembered the saying that if anything sounds too good to be true, it's probably a prize on *Sale of the Century*. So since I now wasn't being paid to be a lady of leisure, there was nothing for it but to head into the office and take Fifi with me. I guessed she might as well get used to the place she would probably inherit one day now that all Russian bets were off. During the day, Fifi would be well looked after by our wonderful nanny, Anna, and I could always comfort her on the spot if she needed me.

No sooner had my Bees started cooing over baby Fifi in the office – which I am pleased to say looked immaculate, no doubt because everyone had been anticipating my arrival for days – than the phones started ringing off the hook. One look at Lulu's grim face told me that on the other end of the line was our most challenging client of all, Teddy Gladhand. The property developer with a portfolio that included shopping centres and boutique hotels was apparently quibbling about our latest invoice. He wanted to cut it down to half of the lousy six-thousand-dollar-a-month retainer he paid us.

The problem with this was that Teddy – a ranga with a red hot temper to match, whose blonde trophy wife Lydia was, at twenty-three, almost a third his age – was such a pain in the arse that he required round-the-clock service. This meant that whatever time zone he was in, he still called us, even if it was the middle of the night in Australia. If he didn't make contact, the calls would be followed by emails, text messages, tweets and messages on Facebook, which came at us non-stop. If he had a loudhailer handy I'm sure he would use that too. He could conservatively be described as manic.

'Hi, Teddy. How's things?' I said brightly, steeling myself for the tirade.

'Where have you been?' he bellered. 'I've been trying to get hold of you for days. I don't think it's very professional of you to run a business and just to be absent from your—'

Interrupting him mid-rant was never easy but it had to be done. 'Teddy, I've been in hospital giving birth to my daughter,' I said.

But Teddy wasn't listening. He was so used to talking over the top of people that he was on a self-imposed two-minute delay. 'It's not good enough, I'm no longer paying you six thousand dollars a month because I don't get that back in service,' he bellowed. 'So many other companies are after my account, including Wilderstein PR.'

'Teddy, I've just had a baby!' I yelled, sending a couple of Queen Bee interns fleeing to the kitchen in fear. 'You know that big belly I was running around with? Well, I wasn't auditioning for *The Biggest Loser* – that was my daughter, Fifi.'

Teddy paused: it seemed that the message had sunk in at last. 'Congratulations,' he said coldly. 'I hope mother and daughter are doing well,' he added mechanically. 'But I'm still not paying your fees.'

For a moment I wished that Ivan and Svetlana really were running the show because then I could have sent Teddy some toxic blinis or something equally exotic. But it was down to me with little back-up to make him see the light. The truth was that although the money was good and constant – plus in the eyes of my accountant it was a blue-chip account – Teddy just wasn't worth the grief.

'You know what?' I told him. 'You can take your arse out of this agency, because life is definitely too short to have to deal with someone like you.'

At that, Teddy went quiet, I shook the phone to see whether the line had dropped out. Teddy usually only oscillated between yelling and really yelling; staying silent was an alien concept for him.

'Don't be so stupid,' he said finally, just before I hung up. 'You know you'll regret this.'

It was true, I did regret many things right now – especially while glancing around the Queen Bee showroom, which, in spite of the Bees' efforts, had been decimated by celebrities borrowing clothes for Fashion Week. But losing Teddy as a client? Not so much. As I moved towards my suspiciously pristine desk, I noticed a rag of a dress hanging forlornly on a rack. What was this – a *Project Runway* reject? Since when did we get that account?

'Oh, that,' said Amy, sounding embarrassed. 'That was borrowed by Lynley Booth, the brand-new fashion editor for *Fashion Style*. She must have been channelling Lindsay Lohan, because that's the way it looked when she returned it. It was once a Kurt Greer sample.'

'Well, we can never return it to Kurt in that state. We'll have to buy it from him,' I said sternly. 'And make sure Victoria Creighton hears about it, because we can't afford to have that happen again.' Victoria was the editor-in-chief at *Fashion Style*.

Amy looked suitably chastened. 'I'm on it,' she said, almost yanking the offending garment off the rack.

'Send Victoria the before and after pictures of that dress,' I said. 'She's going to have to make it up to us.'

With Fifi and her nanny playing happily in the boardroom, watched over by several Bees, I could now turn my attention to other pressing matters.

First up was a proposal that had been put together before Fashion Week to launch Salon, a small label by one of Australia's oldest brands. Now it seemed as though we were about to close the deal, with the brand's marketing director, Myles Woods, requesting an urgent meeting at the end of the week. He was flying in from Melbourne and wanted to meet over lunch. And he wanted that meeting to be with me. The only problem was we had promised him that a certain Sydney identity would be the brand's ambassador. We had already sounded her out but now she had started upping her demands through her hard-assed manager, Aerin, who unfortunately no one had a line on. We would have to close the deal by COB tomorrow or start negotiations with someone totally different.

'And I haven't told you the worst bit,' said Lulu, who still looked slightly flustered by the morning's high drama with Teddy. 'Diane Wilderstein is also going for the account.'

This was not supposed to be the way it would go. Wilderstein PR, hopefully backed by the Shavaliks, were supposed to be keeping busy looking for new accounts – just not any of mine. First Teddy Gladhand was threatening to sign up with Diane and now Salon would be lost to her as well? What the . . . ?

Right, that was all the motivation I needed to pull this coup off. 'Brainstorming session in twenty,' I ordered. 'Tell the troops to assemble in my office. This has to be a group effort – through all of our contacts, we have to find the right celebrity ambassador for Salon, and it has to be someone with the style to make schmutter look as expensive as an important label.'

I began flicking through the latest local magazines to remind myself of the sort of talent that was out there, while Lulu brought up our A-list party guests on her computer screen. The problem was that most of the well-known faces were already linked with other brands, especially the international beauty queens, who may as well have become walking billboards, endlessly spruiking a brand or service.

'Let's look at Chic's Celebrity List,' suggested Lulu. 'At least we know they're managed by someone sensible.'

I could see the rest of the Bees making urgent calls on their mobiles and scrutinising the screens on their computers to come up with a list of likely candidates for Salon. It was cheering they knew me well enough to know that a brainstorming session meant they had to come up with the goods before they took a seat.

I looked up to see Thelma coming towards me, her face pale and anxious. Was there more drama with the Russians? I knew I would have to face them very soon. They just weren't on my to-do list for today.

Thelma, who really did look much younger than her twenty years, appeared mortified at having to interrupt my morning. 'Ah, Jazzy Lou, there's someone waiting to see you in reception, and he won't take no for an answer.'

It was Teddy Gladhand, who had driven in all the way from the north side of Sydney, and negotiated the Harbour Bridge at the tail end of peak hour to try to convince me not to drop his account. He was not only clutching a big bunch of flowers for me, but also made an offer to increase our retainer by four thousand dollars a month. This was unheard of – was Teddy having a nervous breakdown?

'I want that offer in writing before I'll even consider it,' I insisted. 'And you will need to sign a new contract pronto, before you change your mind.'

Teddy started puffing out his chest in the way he did when he was about to explode, but then he miraculously pulled himself back before self-immolation. 'I'm a man of my word and, to be honest, I find your lack of trust mildly offensive, Jazzy Lou.'

'Oh, you want to talk offensive?' I hissed at him, while everyone else suddenly made themselves scarce. 'Your rudeness to my staff is unacceptable,' I said sternly, handing the hapless Thelma the bunch of flowers to plonk in a vase.

'They're David Austin roses – ten dollars a stem. Be careful with them.' Teddy just couldn't help himself; he was such a control freak, he was even trying to assert his authority over a peace offering.

'Teddy!' I shouted, waving a now seriously startled Thelma back to her post as I went on with my counterattack. 'And then there's that seventeen-year-old pest in your office, the amazingly ambitious Chloe, who keeps emailing us to suggest more effective ways that we could promote you. Well, you're welcome to give her free rein – maybe she's a marketing genius – but I don't like your chances, because to tell you the truth everything she comes up with is totally woeful. She sounds like she's spouting Marketing 101 for those who want to run their own cake stall at the local school. Good luck with that.' There it was, I'd finally said it, and for a moment all the sound was sucked out of the room. Blame those leftover pregnancy hormones for making me act as if I'd swallowed a truth serum smoothie.

Teddy's face turned bright red as he stared at me incredulously. So what, he had it coming to him. Right on cue, from inside the meeting/lunch room (not that the Bees ever got time to eat more than a protein bar at their desks) I heard Fifi's cries. She had obviously woken from a nap and since she was in a new, alien environment – an office – I should be the one to go in there to soothe her and give her a bottle, even though Anna was very capable of doing that. It would also make the perfect excuse to end the conversation with Teddy.

'Sorry,' I said, sounding as insincere as I felt. 'Gotta go. Lulu, would you show Teddy out?' And with that I turned and walked towards the boardroom.

'Jazzy Lou, you can't be serious,' Teddy called after me. 'Nobody fires me, and you definitely need me as a client. I'll wait here for you – I know you'll change your mind.'

'Bye, Teddy,' I hollered as I took Fifi from Anna and cuddled her before offering her the bottle. Why the hell did

69

those Russians have to be so shonky? I asked myself for the hundredth time. This was what my life was supposed to be about right now, looking after my baby, not dealing with prima donnas like Teddy, who thought because we were his publicists that he could treat us as though we were dud employees.

Let's just say I was somewhat taken aback when I walked back into the reception area after finally settling Fifi to find Teddy on the couch with a cup of tea in one hand, a pen in the other, and one of our large brainstorming pads on his lap. He looked so sheepish it was almost embarrassing.

Lulu shot me a warning look in case I started laying into him again. 'Jazzy, Teddy and I have been working on a new employment contract,' she said, as if it was the most natural thing in the world to be writing a list of rules of conduct for Attila the Hun.

'Look, I'm sorry about some of the things that have happened in the past, especially about the way Chloe has overstepped the mark,' he said, almost contritely. 'From now on I'll make sure she has nothing more to do with your office.'

This was sounding good.

'And I'll be on my best behaviour,' he promised. 'Now, can you resume work on my account again? And I mean ASAP?'

'Okay,' I agreed. 'We'll give it another shot but you are def on three months' probation. Any more screaming abuse and you will be in our too hard basket, permanently.'

Teddy was clearly the kind of man who needed some tough direction from anyone whom he came in contact with otherwise he would walk all over them. I left it to Lulu to see him out and promised that we would be in touch soon with a new plan of attack.

'As if the morning could not get any more twisted. My personal mobile started to ring and the caller ID recognised Wally Grimes' number from when I'd had to call him at Catalina the other evening. I barely had a moment to wonder how he had got my private number before the line went dead, then it started to ring again. The process was then repeated another three times. It seemed that this bizarre sequence was his way of communicating the fact that this was a top priority call, and I could almost imagine him smacking his fleshy lips together as he pressed redial.

'Yes,' I said flatly when I finally decided to see what he was calling about.

'Oh Jasmine, I do hope I'm not disturbing you,' he crooned, but was unable to hide the venom in his voice. 'So sorry if I woke you. Are you getting any sleep at all since your daughter was born?'

Okay, so no congratulations or anything. Was he hoping to find me a screaming mess after such a momentous occasion in my life? My instincts told me that this call wasn't just about him being able to boast to his ever-diminishing circle of female hyenas how putrid I sounded on the phone and how I was just not coping at all.

I was right.

'Anyway,' he said, when the silence on my end of the line evidently became too uncomfortable to bear, 'when are the christening invitations going out? And is it true that my good friend Pamela Stone is to be the godmother?'

I still didn't bother answering him. As for Pamela being his best friend – puhleese, they hated each other. There was absolutely no one Wally was more wary of than Pamela because he thought he should be the only one everyone talked about. But so what if she was going to be Fifi's godmother? Pamela had been incredibly loyal to me over the years because she respected the fact that I was not afraid to work hard and I had all the time in the world for her.

'Are you still there, Jazzy Lou, or have you fallen asleep on me? Hehehe.' Wally's attempt at a theatrical laugh fell as flat as the way he attempted to work the room at a party, by sashaying around like a reject from the Priscilla, Queen of the Desert auditions.

'Cut to the chase, Wally.' I said, keen to bring the conver- · sation to an end.

'Well, of course, I would like to come. That would be lovely, I'm sure,' he cooed. 'Do you already have a party planner working on it?'

I decided to ignore that in the hope my silence would unnerve him into telling me what he had on his mind. Just taking a call from him was already starting to make me feel queasy. It worked.

'I hear that your Russian partners are trying to sue you for breach of contract,' he said finally. 'And that they have given you an astronomical bill for some furniture that was due to be installed at your headquarters. Is that correct? Would you care to make a comment about that?'

I couldn't help myself, I started to laugh, as much from relief as anything else.

'Why is that so amusing?' he asked suspiciously. 'Has someone else already raised it with you? Is your pathetic little friend Luke Jefferson about to reveal all in his largely unread column?'

Lukey unread? He probably had more readers than the last instalment of the Harry Potter series compared to Wally's readership. Let him think whatever he wanted to – maybe I should call Luke and have a debrief about it all. It was always good to start spinning that kind of story first.

'But Wally,' I said airily, 'how can I be sued for breach of contract when no contract existed in the first place? Now, if you will excuse me, I have a baby girl to look after.'

The next call I made was to my lawyers. 'Wally Grimes has just called me with a story that the Russians are trying to sue Queen Bee for breach of contract?' I said the moment I was transferred through to Marshall Coutts.

'Oh hello, Jasmine, how are you? Motherhood agreeing with you?' Marshall made a point of going through the social niceties because he always accused me of lacking any sort of diplomatic skills when no client was around to pick up the tab.

'Do you know how he found out about that?' I demanded. I had no time to waste on idle chitchat

'Well, we have all the documents here,' Marshall confirmed, 'but I doubt they were leaked from this office. I think you'll find that Ivan himself has probably been tipping everyone off to counter the press release you sent out. Anyway, Jasmine, if he does try to sue you it will make a riveting court case before it is thrown out by the judge.'

If Marshall's comments were meant to comfort me, they had the opposite effect. I was starting to get those old butter-flies in the tummy which I last experienced when I worked for Diane Wilderstein and was summoned to her office to be royally shit-kicked for any number of transgressions – from not picking up her dry-cleaning to not being awake 24/7 to save one of her wacky clients from being made a meal of from the paps. At her peak, Diane refused to acknowledge regular working hours. Even on holidays, our mobiles had to be turned on, so she could contact us if some sort of issue arose. And it always did.

The only thing I knew for sure was that all these potentially long and protracted legal battles were going to cost a great deal of money, so it looked as though we would be taking Teddy up on his offer of increased fees. And we were going to have to become even more hungry for new accounts – I needed to compile a shopping list of the ones that we could land. And first thing tomorrow I would have to sit down with the accountant.

When the next call came through, I absent-mindedly answered it myself. 'Queen Bee,' I said automatically.

'Queen Bee?' the female caller repeated to me. 'I have Tod Spelsen on the line for Jasmine Lewis.'

Tod Spelsen was a fashion designer who was making it huge now in LA, even though he was originally from Australia. This was the label that even the most blase supermodels were desperate to walk for. 'Yes, one moment please,' I replied, trying to sound like my own personal assistant and pressed the loudspeaker button so everyone could hear. Holding the phone out from my ear and shushing my Bees, who had all gathered around when they saw me mouth Tod's name, I walked loudly across the floor so that my heels made a satisfying clip-clop sound.

'Ye-es,' I said in my best Jasmine-Lewis-means-business tone.

What Tod had to say totally floored me. He was travelling to Australia the following week and wanted to set up an appointment with me. Seems he was looking for a PR company down under, and if it all panned out there was a possibility of looking after his business globally.

'I've heard so many good things about you, and I believe that we share the same star sign, Gemini,' he said.

I nodded back, which was really just silly since we weren't on Skype. 'Yes, yes,' I said quickly, losing my last ounce of cool.

'Well then, Miss Lewis, it seems that the planets are aligned! I do have the overwhelming feeling that we're meant to work together. Maybe it's in the stars. I look forward to meeting you in person in your offices next week.'

So Tod Spelsen was a nut job and a bit of a stoner. There was nothing wrong with that, especially with his account one of the most sought after in the world of PR. Now he was personally coming into this office.

I briefly wondered again about taking delivery of all those French antiques that the Russians wanted us to pay for. But they were probably as fake as Ivan's residency permit and Tod would smell them a mile off. Besides, we didn't have the account yet. Instead I decided to call in my event guru, Laurence, who would be able to transform Queen Bee into something witty, sophisticated and suitably cosmic for the international designer – and it was hardly going to cost me a cent, since Laurence owed me big time for helping him save face after some very personal photos of him appeared on a social networking site.

When Fifi and I finally made it home after what had certainly been an action-packed day, Michael didn't seem pleased by my breathless rendition of the day's events.

'I've been thinking that it has all become too much for you,' he said, sadly, when I had cleared away the last of the containers from Dial-A-Dinner Party. 'So I have decided to pay your salary for taking a year off to look after Fifi and me. You could even consult to my company and help us present to our clients better. Couldn't you find someone else to take over the business?' he pleaded. 'What about Lulu?'

He was gazing at me beseechingly with his big blue eyes, the look that was almost guaranteed to make me go weak at the knees. But not tonight, when I was still buzzing from the events of the day.

'Don't be silly, Michael. You won't have to pay me to do that. I intend to make enough for all three of us and I can help you with your business anytime.'

Practically any female-orientated self-help guru would have been able to tell me this is not the way you are supposed to approach your significant other. My Jewish grandmother, Bubbe, would have had me on a toasted bagel if she knew what I had just said. I could just hear her now: 'Nu, you dumbcluck. You always let the man wear the pants in the family – even when you are down to the last pair.'

Michael just stared at me balefully. Then he stood up and walked out of the room. This was the first time ever while we had lived under the same roof that Michael went to sleep in the spare room. It was something of a watershed moment and one I never wanted to repeat.

7

It took all of my chutzpah to be able to hold the launch of edgy fashion magazine and internet site *Point Blank* at Butterworth, the Bellevue Hill mansion of one of Sydney's neediest socialites (well, what didn't she need when it came to milking an occasion for all it was worth?).

The recently separated Ella Von Scandale's husband, Piers, had done the bleedingly obvious and run off with the nanny. If rapidly ageing blonde Ella had been absolutely sure that she would be fairly treated in her divorce settlement, she would never have contemplated opening the doors of Butterworth to people she frankly didn't know and would probably never see again. However, the intel (through the divorce lawyer) was that tyre magnate Piers had already secured their vast fortune in the Canary Islands and would soon be pleading poverty.

Tracking down those assets would take several teams of highly expensive forensic accountants, and in the meantime Ella and her teenage children had to eat. So the hundred grand she was offered for stylists to transfer her home into a French chateau for the launch was quite welcome. Plus she had a clause put into the contract that if any of the props took her fancy, she could keep them. And she wanted a designer gown thrown in as well, since she could hardly face the fashion world in last season's Alex Perry.

Yes, Ella Von Scandale had always understood that timing was everything. She must have been a hell of a lover, because she knew all about withdrawal at the last minute. Each time everyone was just about to stand up from the bargaining table, business concluded, she would find one more condition. The more time I spent in her company, the more I marvelled that her marriage to the flirtatious Piers had lasted as long as it had. Despite his attraction to women of all shapes and sizes, the man was clearly a saint for putting up with the neurotic and demanding Ella. However, Butterworth had several key assets that made it worth my while to be tortured by Ella's prevarications – it had its own polo field and a small maze in the garden, plus it had never been utilised for any sort of launch before. It was just too, too perfect.

Finally an agreement was reached, and thanks to the awesome work by our stylists, Butterworth now looked like it belonged in downtown Fontainbleau, rather than a leafy Bellevue Hill street within jogging distance of Bondi. We also put on extra Bees just for the event, two of them dedicated to ensuring that Ella was plied with champagne and kept pretty much mesmerised by some of the male eye candy on display.

In the countdown to the launch of Point Blank, everything was going to plan. Anya had organised the delivery of the cake from Sweet Art which was an exact replica of the front cover of the magazine and its website. It was to be ceremoniously cut by the magazine house's ambitious, toothy publisher, Gertrude Roberts, who always wanted to be front and centre at any event. We also had the obligatory fireworks display by the same people who were responsible for Sydney's famous New Year's Eve cracker night. Most ambitious of all, Butterworth's famous fountain at the end of the drive had been transformed into a champagne fountain, through a clever visual illusion that made the bubbles look as though they were spurting from the original water jets, when in fact they came out of another device, beautifully lit. The champagne fountain had ended up costing nearly sixty thousand dollars and I was damned if our hostess was going to score that. In fact, I wanted it disassembled once the last of the guests had moved into the marquee erected on the lawn. It was now essentially a Queen Bee prop, which would be used in several more launches this year in very different areas.

With the countdown on, Anya and Emma were stationed at the other end of the driveway with the guest list, which was littered with A-listers and the magazine's key advertisers (those with at least a million-dollar spend).

All week Anya, whose name was on the official RSVP, had been bugged by tragic nobodies trying to talk their way in.

The worst was Sonny Poon, an exotic self-styled CEO from an electronic company that nobody had heard of, who was notorious with other PRs around town for always trying to wangle his way into the hottest event of the week.

'He's just told me that no beautiful people list should be without him as he is also a model,' a giggling Anya had said during the week, putting the phone receiver in a drawer as she regaled the rest of the Queen Bee office with Sonny's latest requests.

This had our internet wiz Alice feverishly hitting the keyboards until she had indeed found a photo of Poon striking a James Bond-style modelling pose with a mobile phone pressed to his ear. But sadly there was no mention of his model agency.

'I'm sorry,' Anya had told Sonny when she retrieved the receiver from the drawer and managed to compose herself, 'but the only models invited are Megan, Jen and Miranda.'

'But you don't understand, I'm a leading member of the Indian community, and the bigwigs behind *Point Blank* will definitely want me there. I'm sure of it.'

'Sorry,' Anya had told him, 'maybe some other time.'

'"Leading member of the Indian community",' she laughed when she'd finally got rid of him. 'Leading wanker, more like it.'

So, would Sonny just turn up tonight and get ready to strike a pose? I didn't like his chances. To deter any would-be gatecrashers, security guards were strategically placed all around the property, but particularly at the entrance. This was an exclusive event and I didn't want any of the guests to look around them and suddenly see one of Sydney's many desperadoes who would turn up to everything from a party in a shop to a book launch.

And while half the city's key influencers were getting styled and polished for tonight's party, I was wearing my usual outfit of choice – a crisp white Givenchy tee, Bassike lowslungs and a skyhigh pair of Laboutin 'Pigalles' – with my freshly washed hair scraped back in a high ponytail. My only concessions to the bling that the occasion demanded of everyone else were my diamond and white gold Chanel watch, a tennis bracelet studded with thirty carat diamonds that had been a special gift from an old friend, and the seven-carat diamond ring that Michael had given me as a push present and which meant we were officially engaged.

Dressed in this very outfit, I was briefing Vogue Williams, the model/DJ wife of Brian McFadden, when an apparition caught my eye that was so darn alarming, I thought I was hallucinating from staying up too long for Fifi's early morning feeds.

Picking her way delicately through Butterworth's cobbled entrance was my old boss and nemesis Diane Wilderstein in all of her Botoxed glory, clutching onto a man with a chiselled jaw, carefully streaked blonde hair and slightly bulgy, clear blue eyes. Yes, my ex-business partner, Ivan Shavalik. My plan had worked and they had found each other but I don't recall seeing either of their names on the invitation list, and just having them there made me feel uneasy.

There was something about Ivan's old fashioned black velvet jacket and tie that made him seem a little dangerous – like the Russian spy in an old James Bond movie. But it was with some satisfaction that I noted that Diane, who was dressed all in black, was wearing last season's YSL Tributes. Or was it the season before. Either way, they looked like a toxic couple and I wondered whether either of them would turn feral when they had a couple of drinks. Ignoring them was sadly not an option, especially because if they had somehow faked an invitation I would have them thrown out with as little fuss as possible. Grabbing a spare guest list from a startled security guard, I marched over to them, but Diane got in before I could utter a word.

'Jasmine, what a surprise to see you here. Don't tell me you're working tonight? Who's looking after your baby?'

I could sense Ivan's penetrating stare, no doubt intended to unnerve me, but I kept focusing on Diane – the way you don't take your eyes off a venomous creature in the bush. 'Her father,' I said evenly. 'Now, is there something I can help you with? This is a private function.'

Diane's beaded Cooper number deemed to rattle with outrage at my question but she smiled as sweetly as she could with her scarlet slash of a mouth that was always, always turned down. 'Not at all,' she demurred. 'Ivan here, whom I believe you know, is a major advertiser in *Point Blank*. You'll notice he has the entire gatefold for Pantheon watches, for which he has the global agency, and naturally he asked me to accompany him. He was worried that a Queen Bee party would be too boring to deal with on his own.'

Of course, I knew that Ivan had the agency for Pantheon but I had not registered the ads properly when I was looking at the launch issue. But why wasn't his name on the invitation list? Knowing him, he had probably not bothered to RSVP and then just shown up.

'Really?' I said, laughing nonchalantly. 'Boring? When I learnt everything from you Diane? How could that be?' I winked at Ivan. 'I hope you both have a wonderful time and now if you will excuse me, I have to look after some other arrangements.'

I could see that Thelma was trying frantically to attract my attention, so we wandered towards a quiet area where we could chat. 'What is it?' I asked the quivering girl in front of me, who looked even more like a nymph with her long hair frizzing up around her face.

'S-s-sorry,' she apologised for being the bearer of potentially bad news, 'but the latest intel is that Ivan has bought into Diane's agency and they've told everyone they're going to win all your accounts and send you broke.'

Of course, the first half was exactly what I had hoped would happen but what was this about trying to steal my accounts and send me broke? There were quite enough accounts in this town for everyone. Besides weren't most of my clients loyal to me? Nobody could match the Queen Bee service because I made sure that we were always available 24/7. Before I could digest this information, I had to deal with a more immediate crisis, which revolved around our talent and their lack of respect for their surroundings. Alec Shadow, the American singer who had just had a number one hit around the world with 'Sleep Walking', was to have been the special guest tonight to perform, but was now apparently holed up in the Park Hyatt with a throat infection. According to his manager, Roscoe, he could hardly speak, let alone sing. Blame it on all those germs floating around the stale air on his flight from the US.

A local artist, Larry Low, who fancied himself as the next Chris Brown, had taken his place at the last minute, and had appropriated one of Butterworth's guest bedrooms as his green room. This had made our charming host Ella Von Scandale very nervous, but not nearly as fraught as she would be after she had a good look at her carpets. At Emma's insistence, when I went to check on Larry, I saw that he had been practising his breakdancing on the white silk carpet and there were black marks all over it from the rubber soles of his trainers. So now Emma was frantically calling the carpet cleaner to see if he could come out in the early hours of the morning at the same time as bump out, when all the settings would be taken away by the stylists. He would no doubt charge three times the usual rate but it would be a drop in the ocean compared to what it would cost if Ella sued us for damages.

With Larry Low's new green room hurriedly moved to the pool cabana, and Ella distracted by Adam Nobbles – winner of two reality shows on television and now a member of the cast of *Sunset Beach* – the situation was almost contained, for now. I could take a moment to silently rage about Diane. There was no way she could take me on, even with all that Russian money – which would be as good as worthless anyway once Immigration caught up with that group. The idea of her basically printing out my client list and trying to take every one on it was not what I had expected when I thought of putting them together. I mean 'what the fuck?' I didn't exactly think she would send me round a bunch of flowers for recommending her in the first place to Ivan but I thought she would play a bit nicer than this. Suddenly the balmy Sydney evening was pierced by a bloodcurdling scream. Ella Von Scandale had just walked into her guest bedroom and taken a look at her carpet. It looked as though a graffiti artist armed with some black greasy paint had run amok in there and no amount of emergency carpet cleaning was going to make a difference.

8

The launch got more exposure in the next day's gossip columns than we could ever have hoped for – it just wasn't the kind of publicity we wanted. Even my BFF, Luke Jefferson, breathlessly reported in his column in *The Sun* that guests attending the launch of *Point Blank* at society pitstop Butterworth had at first thought that someone must have committed a murder at the historic Sydney mansion (which would have no doubt only added to its lustre).

Swept along on a small ocean of champagne bubbles, a story had gathered momentum that Ella Von Scandale had discovered at least one body, and maybe two – so piercing were her screams when she walked in and found her white silk carpet ruined. Adam Nobbles, whose arm was at the time wrapped possessively around her Alex Perry-corseted waist, at first assumed that her husband had turned up unexpectedly, and was quite shaken. The romantic interlude Ella had planned with the young thespian, whose acting skills would have undoubtedly come in handy in her glamorous bedroom, was also put on hold. Nothing put Ella Von Scandale less in the mood for sex than the prospect of having one of her assets devalued.

Several of her frenemies later remarked that this was where her obvious lack of breeding showed her up. A member of one of Sydney's fast-diminishing group of old-money families would·have only lost the plot behind closed doors; Von Scandale, who had just stopped short of graduating from the appropriately named Rooty Hill High, continued to wail like a banshee.

Some of the more inebriated guests had thought that her cries heralded the start of a new facet of the evening's entertainment – like when they rolled back the doors at the Cointreau Ball to reveal a fleet of dodgem cars (even, one year, dodgem boats).

I had tried to calm her down as best I could, while Adam Nobbles (who had, prior to this interruption, been imagining himself flying to LA at the pointy end of a plane with his new benefactress by his side, and was mentally planning his first hosted lunch at the Soho Club) raced off to get her another glass of champagne. However, the mood was broken. From that moment on she would always associate him with disaster and ruin. Sex was well and truly off the menu.

After that, the night had gone downhill for Point Blank, with some guests leaving before the fireworks. The only saving grace was that it was definitely one of the most memorable parties of the month so far, which was exactly what the magazine's executives had wanted – well, sort of.

For several weeks afterwards, everyone involved handballed the cost of the new white silk carpet for Butterworth. The insurance company tried to put it on the event company for acting irresponsibly by not accompanying the entertainment into the house, and then the event company tried to get the magazine to pay. Of course, the carpet was handmade, and Ella Von Scandale insisted that the entire room had to be done and perhaps the entrance hall as well. 'I simply cannot live any sort of life on a carpet which has been patched,' she declared.

For a while there, it looked as though Queen Bee would have to foot the bill, but the insurance company finally caved in and came good. Ella Von Scandale had done massively well from the night – a big fat fee for loaning Butterworth, a couture gown by Alex Perry which was worth a good fifteen grand, a new white silk carpet, and she somehow managed to hold on to all the leftover wine and champagne too. Von Scandale definitely had balls, just not Adam Nobbles' slightly inflamed ones.

And on that note, the other talking point of the night involved the eastern suburbs property developer, Rick Conrads, who picked up something a little extra when he took home Antonia Brown, fringe TV presenter, who was unfortunately as ambitious as she was largely unwatched. Despite this fact she managed to borrow an Allison Palmer gown from the showroom to wear to the launch of Point Blank because she insisted to Lulu that she had a TV crew following her around that night. And sure enough, there was one lone cameraman who looked as though he was filming on something resembling his iPhone but with a tiny tripod attached to it. This had kept many of the Bees amused at the start of the night; Antonia's cameraman was so intent on filming her, you would have sworn it was David Attenborough shooting a wildlife doco. The Bees especially loved it when he walked backwards with his iPhone trained on her and they screamed at him that he was about to take out the champagne fountain. Antonia hardly blinked, entirely focused on sucking in her heavily made-up cheekbones and staring moodily into the distance in front of the photo wall. This was just as well, because none of the photographers was calling out her name – in fact, all that could be heard from the lensmen was a faint muttering: 'Who's that again? Is she anyone? Oh ta, I didn't think so.' (The local paps are the best social barometer in Sydney; if they hardly bother to lift their cameras, it's clear that the person standing in front of them has hardly any celebrity currency at all. And when that happens, it's best to pretend you had dropped something on the red carpet rather than trying to pose on it.) Antonia was so thick-skinned she could have stood in for a crocodile on the Discovery Channel. She just kept on posing up a storm for her own 'lensman' as if she was Angelina Jolie at the Oscars. That was until she spotted Rick Conrads arriving in head to toe Gucci and sidled up to him immediately, gesturing behind her back for the hapless photographer to scram. Luckily for her, Rick was in a particularly flirtatious mood that night so she was quickly able to monopolise his attention. By the time that Ella Von Scandale made her scene, Rick and Antonia were ready to slip away. There was so much going on that not even gossip columnist Pamela Stone had clocked them because she was so distracted by whatever was up with Ella Von Scandale. She was scurrying towards those screams in order to be first on the scene with her video camera turned on. Pamela was fearless when it came to tracking down a story.

At least the earth had moved for someone that night. It was just darned unfair that a few days later Rick was spotted making a beeline for a certain Double Bay practice where the doctor was not only ultra knowledgeable but also extremely discreet. He needed to be, because Rick had noticed a discharge from his penis following his night of unbridled lust with Antonia. Naturally, the doctor didn't divulge to Rick that he was actually not the first to pick up something from that source: Antonia was a walking STD epidemic. Naturally, the word spread quickly back to the Queen Bee office and it was resolved never to lend Antonia another outfit again, particularly not a gown by Allison Palmer.

In fact, for the next few days everyone was banned from borrowing from the Queen Bee showroom except for bona fide fashion editors and stylists for big-name stars. We needed to do a stocktake because it looked as though we were about to land a huge new client.

Tod Spelsen had followed up his call with a series of emails about his possible visit to Australia to talk to Queen Bee about the release of Spelt, his own scent and beauty line which he wanted to launch in his home country before taking it to the rest of the world.

Tall and deeply tanned, Spelsen's trademark was his mop of tight dark curls which he somehow just managed to keep under control. So extreme was this hairstyle that it gave 'Kaiser' Karl Lagerfeld and his signature platinum ponytail a run for its money. Like Karl, Tod had dressed everyone from Marie-Chantal, Crown Princess of Greece, to Kelly Osbourne; they were all fans of his immaculate tailoring that managed to look both quirky and sexy. There was never any mistaking a Tod Spelsen design and, although plenty tried to copy them, no one was ever fooled by the imitations. Everyone was excited about working on the account, and Lulu in particular had been pulling ideas together for the pitch ever since he made that first call. His visit to our office would definitely be a 'moment'. So it was a real downer when we learnt that Tod could not make it home right at this time anyway, and that the project would be put on hold. Put on hold? No one puts Jasmine Lewis in the back catalogue. Some sort of affirmative action had to be taken.

As it happened, I had been thinking of taking a trip to LA with my oldest friend, Shelley Shapiro, to find my wedding gown because Michael and I had now set the date. (We decided that there would never be a right time to marry, so we should schedule it in and hope for the best. There had been an unexpected Sunday opening at Quay, so a celebrant had been booked and the wedding invites were being sorted. What could go wrong?)

For shopoholic Shelley, a trip to LA was a lifeline because she had been away from her favourite stores for far too long. She had started waking in a sweat in the middle of the night murmuring 'Giorgio Armani, Chanel, Barneys, Neiman's'. This trip to LA was her equivalent of a pilgrimage to mecca (not the beauty stores but the holy site). Shelley and I had been good buddies ever since we had attended the same private school and had repeatedly found ourselves in trouble. She was bright, fearless and a couple of clothing sizes ahead of her classmates. Brought up in a single parent family, her mum was particularly lenient but she sadly passed away just before Shelley's eighteenth birthday. This left Shelley with her own home and a big, fat inheritance, so now she was a Trustafarian who dabbled in property development. Her main occupation, which she playfully noted on Visa documentation was 'shopper'. But Shell hated to be seen in the same outfit twice, which was great for me because she continually gifted them to me along with the ones that she never wore. This was because she suffered from an unfortunate case of body dysmorphia – she was a gorgeous size four but in her mind, she was a zero.

'Sweetie, I can't believe that we are finally having a girls' day out,' she cried down the line, when I told her about the LA trip. 'You owe me so many of these that we'll be gone for around a month, right?'

'Wrong, less than a week,' I responded with a big grin on my face. Shelley had a way of making everything seem like an hilarious escapade. She was like a Darren Star version of a fairy godmother. In fact the *Sex and the City* creators could build an entire mini-series around my mate, Shell — and it was sure to be a winner.

Fifi was far too tiny to come on this escapade with us but she would be well taken care of at home by Anna and her two grandmothers, along with Michael before he went back to Asia on business.

Michael wasn't too excited about it but, since he couldn't really come shopping with me for a wedding dress and he had to be in Beijing for meetings, he accepted it — although the thought of my travelling companion made him a bit nervous. 'You're taking Shelley,' he pointed out, 'and you know how you two love to party.'

'Not anymore,' I said sternly. 'I'm a mother now.'

My trip to LA would also be the perfect opportunity to present our proposal to Tod. I was genuinely excited by the idea of launching Spelt, which was fast becoming one of the hottest labels in the world. Another Australian great, design king Marc Newson, had created the deeply sexy packaging for Spelt's beauty lines, and it was well on its way to becoming a cosmetic icon, taken up by the top echelon of fashion bloggers and influencers. We had already started to plan the launch into Australia, which would include staging a fashion show like no other at a top-secret and controversial venue. Sydney's blasé fashion set wouldn't know what had hit them. They would be sitting on the edge of their seats – the setting would be so startling that, at least for the first few minutes, everyone would totally forget to reach for their iPhones. Then Instagram would go into meltdown. I wanted to stage the entire show around Rubica, the Australian model of the moment, who was currently working in Paris. At the show's finale, Amazonian male and female models dressed only in glistening body paint would distribute Marc Newson-designed cosmetic satchels to the crowd. This would be the show that everyone would talk about for the rest of the year, and I was hoping to do it at a reasonable budget. Perhaps many of the event and production people would be so taken with being a part of the Spelt launch that they would offer their services at a greatly reduced price. The whole launch had been so well planned that I hoped to lay out everything in front of Tod and his advisers, including the shots of the location, the models and even the guest lists for the launch. It was like a true military exercise in the war against fashion boredom, and I was very proud of it.

But when the call finally came through from LA, let's just say it wasn't the one that I was expecting. Lulu answered, and I could tell immediately from the frown on her face that something was up.

'You had better tell Ms Lewis that yourself,' she said, shortly after taking the call, and handed the receiver to me.

'Hello? Yes, this is Jasmine Lewis,' I confirmed to the dreaded Jenna Katz, Tod Spelsen 's humourless American PA. 'Are you calling to confirm our meeting?'

There was a silence on the line – the kind of vacuum that can just suck all the energy out of you and leave you with a sense of foreboding.

'I'm afraid not, Ms Lewis. Tod has asked me to say thank you for your efforts but he has now decided to go with another Sydney publicity company. However, he would like to keep all of your details on file and, should another opportunity come up, Queen Bee will be the first one he calls.'

I swallowed hard. 'Excuse me, what?' I was flabbergasted. I glanced at Lulu, who looked sick. What could have influenced Tod to make such a sudden decision? Had news of Ella Von Scandale's ruined white carpet reached LA? Surely not.

'Just to clarify the situation, Tod is using someone else,' said Jenna Katz who seemed to be enjoying her power in imparting such devastating news.

'Who is it?' I blurted out.

Jenna probably shouldn't have told me but apparently she couldn't help herself. 'Wilderstein Public Relations,' she announced with a hint of satisfaction.

WTF? Lulu looked as though she was about to burst into tears as I put down the receiver, having sweetly thanked Jenna for taking the time to make the call. (There was no way I was going to give her the satisfaction of knowing that she had rocked my world.)

What inducements could Diane Wilderstein have offered the uber-stylish Tod Spelsen to get him over the line? Surely she and Ivan did not have what it takes to pull off such an important launch. What would be their big idea: a lunch for the beauty and fashion editors at Rockpool Bar and Grill? Diane's time of being a creative powerhouse were long gone.

'I mean, has he even Googled her?' I asked as Lulu nodded her head in wonderment. 'Diane's still wearing her original acid brights from the eighties. She doesn't understand that fashion has already moved full circle since then.'

What to do?

In times of great calamity, it pays to listen to your inner GPS, and right now the voice inside my head was telling me to go for it anyway. I had nothing to lose by continuing with my plans to fly to LA. There was always the possibility that if I could get in to see Tod and personally show him Queen Bee's impressive blueprint for his launch, he would come to his senses. I just had to hope that he didn't steal any of our ideas and give them to Diane Wilderstein. But surely he had only got as far as he had in life by acting with some integrity? And, besides, doing something like that would just be bad karma.

Meanwhile, I would be able to buy my wedding gown and take a well deserved breather from all the drama and intrigue of the Sydney fashion industry. Short of becoming a Tibetan monk and hiding out in a remote cave (which my Bubbe would basically kill me for), a trip to LA on a shopping expedition for a wedding gown was pretty much it. In the days before our departure, the details of the deal came through on the PR grapevine. Tod Spelsen had signed up Diane Wilderstein because Ivan had had vowed to get the American luxury line into the lucrative Russian market (which had become the promised land for anyone with a luxury product to sell).

The kicker was that Tod would have to hand over all the international PR contracts to Wilderstein PR (well, good luck with that). I was all for Diane taking the Shavaliks off my hands, but not one of my exciting, potential clients as well. It was a good thing that I liked a challenge. I could get a new pitch together in the time it took for Diane to return to the office from one of her signature boozy lunches.

On the eve of my departure to the US, there was even more bad news. We lost two more accounts to Diane, Polar Sunglasses and Fizzy Green Tea. She was welcome to them, because their budgets were so low that pretty much all Queen Bee could do for them was to add them as products in A-list goodie bags. Unfortunately, the chances of an A-lister even putting on a pair of Polars, let alone being snapped in them in public, were roughly the same as Kyle Sandilands becoming the next ambassador for Bonds undies. Polars were about $300 too cheap and had no designer hook up. Sometimes clients presented themselves to Queen Bee and expected us to perform miracles for them but then they refused to take our advice, which was pretty much like insisting on the buffet breakfast option at a restaurant and then just eating the toast.

9

The Four Seasons Hotel on Doheny Drive, Beverly Hills, was one of the places I stayed in LA when The Peninsula had no rooms left. Let everyone else battle with the dim lighting at the SLS, the too-cool-for-school rooms at the Mondrian and, of course, the distressed boho style of the Chateau Marmont, I liked the Four Seasons' old-style glamour. Plus it was a favourite of the visiting stars, with most of the international film junkets taking place within the property. I even loved the smell of the Four Seasons, especially when I walked into the lobby and took in the massive floral displays in all of the public rooms; on top of that, every suite had Bvlgari fragrances.

Once we were all settled and unpacked, with Shelley in the adjoining room to mine, it was time to try and talk some sense into Tod Spelsen. It was all very well being hooked into the Russian market, but did Tod really want to owe his success to the mafia through his new besties Ivan and Svetlana. It was a tricky predicament for everyone including me, because if I leaked stories to the media about their troubles with Immigration, I risked them coming after me. Diane had been supposed to keep them busy so they wouldn't bother about Queen Bee, but not so frenetic that they decimated our business. I wondered how I could delicately convey some of the potential danger to Tod. But then I also wondered how I was going to get to Tod at all with his energetic minder, Jenna Katz, ready to pounce on any unauthorised callers.

I organised with the Four Seasons concierge, Rick, to send a beautiful floral arrangement in Tod Spelsen's signature colours of cream and mint with an invitation to meet at the hotel for a coffee. I wrote the short note to him myself in Mont Blanc fountain pen, because style is of course everything when communicating with a design star. On the note, I advised him that I would call later to arrange a time and was very much looking forward to catching up.

So far, so good. In the meantime, I also asked the hotel to organise a Mercedes convertible for Shelley and me to rent so that we could go bridal shopping much faster.

'And make sure it has a big trunk,' Shelley shouted when I was on the phone to the front desk, 'because I plan to give my black Amex such a workout, I might almost wear it out.'

This sounded so ominous that I wondered whether Rodeo Drive might be prepared for what was about to hit it. According to Shelley, I should have hired a pantechnicon instead of a

Merc convertible but, hell, we could always have her shopping delivered to the hotel if we couldn't fit it in our ride.

Waiting around for a meeting has never been my strong point. I prefer to dive straight in, but the timing on this one had to be perfect – I wanted to give Tod enough time to be wowed by the flowers and digest the news that I had flown in to see him in spite of the fact that he'd turned us down. He had to be flattered by that, right?

Lulu had also lined up a meeting for me with Rufus, a boutique talent agency in Beverly Hills, who were interested in hooking up with an Australian PR company, project by project. The whisper was that global reality star Chelsea Ware, who plays Kitty, the sexsational tampon heiress from the hit series *The Bel Air Life*, was going to be releasing her first album and was embarking on a worldwide publicity tour. I was such a fan of *The Bel Air Life* – best described as *Sex and the City* meets posh Bel Air – that I wanted to take a tour of the places where it was shot.

The man I was meeting at Rufus was Eric Lacey, and a quick check on his Facebook and Twitter postings suggested that he was not only out every night but at several different upscale events with his celebrity clients in the space of just a few hours. LA is a town where appearances are paramount, so I decided that the meeting called for a brand-new outfit. When our car finally arrived, Shelley and I headed straight to Barneys. We didn't even have to ask directions; the car almost drove itself to Wilshire Boulevard.

'I fucking love LA,' Shelley sang out as the warm wind lifted her hair back off her shoulders. 'Once we have done our first round of shopping, we are taking this little baby and heading down Sunset Boulevard because I won't really believe that I am here until I have sunk my first voddie cocktail at Skybar. And they better have that one with acai berries because I am going to be extra healthy this trip, I promise.'

'Of course,' I said as I swung the car into Barneys' service area, nearly wiping out an entire family of Japanese shoppers with my action. 'You've got to look great in your bridesmaid gown.'

'Shit, I'm glad you reminded me,' said Shelley, smacking her thighs. 'Maybe I'll go on the voddie cocktail diet. Someone here is sure to have written a book about it.'

Several hours later, we returned to the hotel, ridiculously elated over our purchases, which meant that we had basically ransacked Barneys' designer floors. Pity that the news when I eventually called Tod Spelsen was so dire. Jenna primly informed me that yes, he had received the flowers thank you very much, but he felt there was no point in seeing me at this time.

So that was that. I was sure if I could get past Tod's guard dog Jenna and speak to the designer directly I could talk him into at least seeing me. This probably meant calling first thing in the morning or late in the evening after she went home, because during the rest of the day she seemed to have control of his mobile phone. Blame it on jet lag, but I almost felt like bursting into tears at the rejection, and I couldn't call Michael because he was on his way to Beijing. Some familiar feelings of inferiority threatened to overcome me. Who was I kidding, I told myself, I'm not cut out for PR. I'm just not smart enough. The thing about those kinds of feelings is that they never last, especially not with Shelley around. No sooner had I started moping about my inability to do my job than she was dialling up the craziest assortment of dishes from room service, while also pleading with them to procure her some Reese's Peanut Butter Cups as there were none in the mini bar.

The main problem was that both of us were feeling jet lagged, so frazzled that we were in danger of falling asleep before the room service waiter had even knocked on the door. All I remember was that some time in the early hours of the morning I woke up to the scent of transfats from our all-American feast of club sandwiches, burgers and fries (so much for Shelley's vow to eat healthy), much of it left uneaten. I managed to roll the trolley out into the hallway, drank a bottle of water and went straight back to sleep. By the time I woke up again, I was back to my upbeat self.

The Rufus agency turned out to be right opposite the Neiman Marcus and Saks department stores in Beverly Hills, almost where we were shopping yesterday, which was handy for Shelley, who could resume thrashing the plastic while I went to meet with the very social Eric Lacey.

I was a little concerned at first to find that Rufus had its own building, because I had thought the agency was a little more niche than that. But in my Ksubi skirt, mixed with a Josh Goot print tee and a Converse high-top, I was pretty sure I had nailed the LA look, which was really the Bondi hipster look to the power of six.

Eric, a tall, red-haired thirty-something man in a sleek Zegna suit and Hermès tie, came to meet me himself in Rufus's chic reception area and almost bowled me over with the strength of the cologne he was wearing. The heavy fragrance seemed to suck all of the oxygen out of the space, but I recovered enough to be ushered into a boardroom where a girl in a T-shirt and denim skirt introduced herself as his assistant, Louise. She looked fresh-faced as if she'd just left college, and she had the kind of style to suggest that she was far too busy and important to think about fashion. I had been expecting that everyone from Rufus would look as though they belonged on the set of *Entourage*.

Once we had done with the pleasantries, Eric fixed me with his intense blue eyes (did he wear special contacts? I wondered). 'We've seen a lot of the work you've done,' he announced, 'and I think you could be just the person to launch this particular reality star down under. Now, have you ever heard of Chelsea Ware?'

So it was true? Lulu's intel was spot on as usual.

'Have I? She's practically the only reason I watch *The Bel Air Life*,' I responded. 'Oh my God, she's fantastic!'

A beaming Eric outlined the proposal, which would include Chelsea's trip to Australia next month to launch her first single. There would be a proper launch party with all of the young

A-listers in attendance and as many TV and radio spots as we could muster. It was the kind of project that Queen Bee would revel in. 'But there's just one thing,' Eric continued. 'Even before we sit down to crunch numbers on it all, Chelsea will want to meet you. She needs to know that your chakras are all, ahem, aligned.'

Of course, she does, I thought. Chelsea did not want to have dozens of hapless PR interns slaving away on her behalf. She needed to know that I was basically not a bitch. I was certainly not any tougher than anyone else who headed up their own company, but I had my bad days that's for sure. And as for seeing a more spiritual side of life, I just didn't have time at the moment to fit it into my schedule – along with the emergency spray tans, the blow dries and the fortnightly eyelash job. Plus I had Fifi and Michael to look after; I just didn't have time to lurk around in the third dimension, looking for the inner me. I noticed that Eric and Louise were studying my face, probably to see whether I could handle a full-blown Californian reality star. Or maybe they were checking whether my chakras looked dodgy. Who knows, maybe they scanned them on the way in? I wondered how much time it would take to get an emergency chakra workout and where the hell they might do that in this town. I was pretty sure it wasn't on the spa menu at the Four Seasons. Hell, when it came to treatments in LA, the only specialist I wanted to see was the Botox doctor to the stars in Santa Monica. I was sure that this trip had already given me extra expression lines. At this rate I was going to look like a forty-year-old by the time I touched down in Sydney again.

'Of course,' was all I said, smiling sweetly and trying hard to exude the air of someone who regularly dined at Urth Caffe. Eric stood up and extended his hand to me, while Louise scurried out the door, only to return seconds later with a box wrapped in lurid purple paper. 'We'll be in touch,' Eric said warmly, 'and you may need this.' Louise handed the box over to me with a little smile on her face that gave nothing away.

'It's an aura spray,' Eric explained. 'It helps to balance your chakra number four – harmony.'

All the way down in the lift, I wondered whether good old Eric really thought that was what I needed. He could be right about that. By the time we reached the ground floor I had already had my first spray of harmony and felt it was time to find my wedding gown. Shelley had been texting me different styles she'd seen at Monique Lhuillier, but I had my heart set on a gown from Vera Wang I had seen the day before when Shelley was having her Goyard moment. I had asked the salesgirls to put it aside for me. Still, there was no harm in looking at her suggestions.

Shelley's choice at Monique Lhuillier was a corseted top and skirt, which I kind of loved. 'It's gorgeous and you're right, it's very me,' I said after I tried it on. 'But I also want to show you something I saw yesterday at Vera Wang.'

Perhaps the staff at America's top bridal designer have become a little blasé about people coming to spend tens of thousands of dollars on a wedding dress, because they seemed a tad casual in their approach. However, after one of their wedding gowns received a global audience of millions thanks to Kim Kardashian's ill-fated marriage to Kris Humphries, maybe they don't get excited by 'civilian' shoppers. (I got that from Joan Rivers, who refers to all non-celebs as civilians.) But when I finally stepped out in the dress, which just happened to be almost the same one that Kim Kardashian had worn during her wedding ceremony, Shelley burst into tears. I had suddenly morphed into the full princess bride.

'It's so beautiful,' she said, her voice shaking. 'It's definitely the one.'

Both of us took photos of the dress and we kept high-fiving each other. Then all that was left to do was to choose the colour for the bow on the waist, pay the money and organise to return for another fitting in three weeks' time, which would mean another trip to LA. Michael was going to be thrilled about that (not), but then he is always telling me about the importance of putting extra effort into everything and getting it right. Besides, if I didn't manage to get Tod across the line on this trip, I would surely do it on the return. Have to think positive.

Before Shelley and I returned to the hotel, we staged a toy-buying expedition for Fifi. My favourite purchase was a lush elephant with his trunk up. Actually I bought it as much for myself as my daughter because something told me we were going to need at least one lucky talisman for the few weeks ahead.

10

There was a note waiting for me back at the hotel, but once again it wasn't the one I had been hoping for. Tod Spelsen hadn't finally come to his senses and decided to see me after all; instead it was from Eric Lacey. It simply said, *Dinner tonight at the Chateau Marmont at 7.30 to discuss all things Chelsea.*

Eric made no mention of whether the reality star would be there or not. However, since it wasn't an invitation so much as a command, I had no alternative but to look in my closet for something to wear in order to fit in at the superstar hangout, where those without any sort of Hollywood pedigree or connections are seated inside the dimly lit restaurant while the real action takes place outside in the courtyard. In the end, I opted for a pair of J Brand jeans, Balenciaga heels and a Kenzo sports deluxe top. Perfect.

I left Shelley the Merc and took the Four Seasons town car, a chauffeured Rolls, giving the driver a twenty-dollar tip to take me to Chateau Marmont – but of course no one saw me arrive in style because the driveway at the raffish hotel is so steep that the drop-off is on Sunset Boulevard. Only the members of Led Zeppelin had been outrageous enough to ride their bikes right into the reception area in a 'fear and loathing' moment right out of the seventies.

Eric and Louise were already seated at one of the courtyard tables when I arrived and had almost demolished their vodka cocktails, but there was a pristine one waiting for me and I couldn't wait to get into it. Hey, it had already been a life-changing kind of day – what with finding the gown I would be wearing to my wedding. It was still early but the place seemed pretty well packed. There was no way I could scout for stars: I need to be cooler than that – even though the blonde who had almost sent me flying as she pushed past when I walked in looked remarkably like Lindsay Lohan. Was she banned from the Marmont or back in as a valued guest? I couldn't remember. Asking Eric and Louise to fill me in on the crowd would have been tacky, so I resisted that as well, but from Eric's constant waves and smiles over my shoulder, it looked like he knew everyone, as might be expected from a big shot agent. Was it just coincidence that he had positioned me at the table with my back to the action?

'Thank you for joining us,' said Eric, who had shed his sleek 'Ari Gold' Zegna suit for an Armani shirt and jeans – not quite hip enough for the Chateau Marmont crew but serious enough to show that he was, after all, there on business. Louise was dressed in something that looked as though it had been snapped up in a Banana Republic end-of-season sale. It told me that she was very low down in the pecking order at Rufus – definitely not enough of a deal to earn a decent pay cheque. As I was always reminding my Bees, in our industry, clothes say it all; it is way better to be dressed in investment pieces than something from a chain store which will last a season at the most.

Eric, Louise and I chewed the fat for twenty minutes as I filled them in on some of the social highlights of Sydney (they were both threatening to come down for the CD launch), when all of a sudden I could sense a seismic shift in the atmosphere in Chateau Marmont's courtyard garden. It was as if all the wannabes there had suddenly sucked in their breath and then erupted as they excitedly informed each other that the outrageous reality star of *The Bel Air Life*, Chelsea Ware (whose real name I later discovered was the less exotic Mindy Reid), had just walked in. All those heads swivelled around in unison when the curvy, delectable blonde sashayed right up to our table. Good old Eric leapt to his feet faster than a Sydney gatecrasher at a black tie dinner who has just noticed a couple of beefy security guards heading his way. He was swiftly followed by Louise, and I rose too, pulling out my chair right onto a passing waiter's foot. It was definitely not one of my finer moments.

'Chelsea!' exclaimed Eric, whose blue eyes I swear had moved up a couple of notches in brightness. (Did contact lenses come with an intensity switch in La La Land? If so, his were now on high beam.) 'Do you have a moment to join us?' he asked, seizing Chelsea by one of her undernourished arms.

'This,' he said, gesturing to me and catching me out gingerly lowering myself into my seat ready to bob up at once should the situation call for it, 'is the Australian publicist Louise and I met with this morning, Jasmine Lewis.' With my bottom now half suspended in the air, I gave good old Chelsea a healthy Aussie wave. Trying to shake hands with her in this position would have just looked wrong, but it was amazing how much LA brought out the Aussie in me. I had started to feel like one of the cast from *Crocodile Dundee* with my retarded mannerisms.

If everyone at the table had been waiting for Chelsea to tell us to please be seated, I swear we would all still be in position, me with my bum all but airborne, but, thankfully, Louise came to her senses first and promptly plonked herself down. We all followed suit while a couple of waiters brought chairs for Chelsea and the tall, blonde Englishwoman with her, who seemed to be a minder. She was later introduced to us as 'Rita', with no other explanation given.

'I can only stop for a couple of minutes because I have an important assignation in one of the bungalows,' Chelsea said, winking at Eric.

My mind ran wild. Who or what was waiting in one of the famed Marmont VIP suites? Maybe the hotel's owner himself, André Balazs, who wanted to host a party for her. Or might it be John Mayer, who was rumoured to have helped out on her CD? Probably the only way I would know for sure was by asking one of the paps at the end of the driveway. They always knew what was going on and were not at all shy in relaying it.

Chelsea now turned her full attention on me. She wanted to know whether many people in Sydney knew of *The Bel Air Life* and whether they liked her or not.

'Of course,' I assured her. 'You're our favourite character from the show, and I promise you that when you visit Sydney you'll be swamped by several brands, no doubt ready to pay you serious money to Instagram their products.'

This made Chelsea Ware smile and it was good to see that, despite her fame, she was as motivated by making money as the rest of us. So much for all the hocus pocus about the chakras, but perhaps that would come later?

'Put it this way,' I told her, 'as far as Queen Bee looking after you in Australia is concerned, it'll be a win/win situation for all of us.'

Another slight shift in the atmosphere told me that another famous person had graced the Chateau Marmont with their presence. Was it Sam Worthington, whom Lulu had informed me was booked into a suite there? (Perhaps he and Chelsea were dining together in the villa?) But no, I nearly spat out my olive pip when I saw that the tall handsome man who had just walked in, his dark mane freshly coiffured, was none other than the man I had come to LA to see, Tod Spelsen. Even more hilarious was the fact that he was led to an adjacent table to ours. However, Tod, who was accompanied by several other men (including one who seemed to be his boyfriend, judging by his proprietorial air), appeared reluctant to sit down straight away, instead hesitating beside our table.

He nodded to Eric, who blanked him – clearly there was no love lost there – while Rita coolly nodded to him, and then finally, in desperation, Tod's eyes rested on me. Perhaps he recognised me from the press cuttings he had been sent during the course of the past few weeks. He certainly didn't address me by name, however it was obvious that he wanted an introduction to Chelsea. I should have looked away and left him squirming, but he was a fellow Aussie after all. I would just have to get to the bottom of what had gone down between him and Eric later on; I guessed it was some kind of dispute over a star not getting the right gown for a red carpet event.

'Hello, Tod,' I said loudly, as though he was hearing impaired – just put it down to overcompensating because of my nerves. 'I'm Jasmine Lewis – hope you liked the flowers I sent you today.'

For a moment or two Australia's most famous export to LA since Nicole Kidman looked perplexed. Then he seemed to realise that I was the one he had pretty much done the dirty on. 'Ah, yes, I was just going to have my assistant call you so we could set up a meeting and talk business,' he said suavely. Yeah right, me and Jenna were absolute besties on the phone. Then Tod turned to Chelsea, who was regarding him with an expression on her face that said 'what a wanker'.

'I don't believe we've met,' he said. 'I'm Tod Spelsen and I'm a big fan of yours. I'd absolutely love it if we could send you some of our clothes.'

Chelsea looked bored. 'Lovely,' she said flatly. 'I'll have someone call you,' and then she turned her back on him before he could introduce the very effeminate man standing next to him whom I'd picked as his boyfriend. I discovered later that Chelsea had been trying to pull off some kind of exclusive deal with Dior, which she did not wish to jeopardise by wearing another designer's clothes to high profile events.

Tod was left staring blankly at me. He was clearly floored by this very public rebuff. I should have been more gracious and somehow put him at his ease, but I allowed myself the smallest smirk. Suck that up, Tod baby, and maybe next time you might take my calls.

11

The Queen Bee office was reality-star central with plans well under way for Chelsea Ware's visit to Sydney and Melbourne next month. She had already been locked in to guest edit *Point Blank* and there was going to be a live performance in the Martin Place studio of *Sunrise*.

But while one part of the office was thriving, our established client base was being seriously depleted, as one by one some of our best accounts were jumping ship.

'What did Hugo from Lou Jeans have to say before he announced he was leaving?' I asked Lulu when I had come up for air again after the trip to LA.

'Just that it was time for a change,' she said quietly. 'I told him we would put a new account director on but he wouldn't play ball.'

Just a couple of days later it all became clear when the trade press announced several new additions to Wilderstein PR's client list. Yes, at least ten of our clients had found a new home with her. The word in the industry was that Diane's fees were undercutting everyone, and she was also offering Russian investment money and the possibility of her clients entering one of the biggest markets of all. It was no wonder so many brands were leaving us, because the financial climate could only be described as hazardous. But the big mystery was how Diane would handle so many clients without the staff and the PR intelligence to deal with them. Admittedly, few could beat the old girl in her day, but too many long lunches washed down with several vineyards of red wine had addled her brain. Unfortunately, we didn't have to wait long to find out how she would manage.

The first resignation letter was slipped into my letterbox at home by Imogen some time in the early hours of the morning. Just to ensure I had received it, Imogen sent me a text message alerting me to the fact that I had mail.

'I just wanted you to know as soon as possible so you could find a replacement,' she said in the office later that day, looking shamefaced but insisting she would be leaving at the end of the week in lieu of the holidays she had not yet taken.

According to her resignation letter, she was leaving to go on a working holiday to London, but there must have been some mistake because the local PR update, *Patsy's News*, had listed her as moving from Queen Bee to Wilderstein PR. I had Imogen escorted from the office just half an hour later, clutching her termination cheque in her hand and her belongings in a cardboard box. And, no, I would not be giving her a reference.

No sooner had Imogen left the building than Yaz, another of my once-loyal Bees, asked to see me and sheepishly gave me her letter of resignation.

'I understand that the timing isn't ideal for you, but I'm leaving on an overseas trip at the end of the month and when I return I want to take the next steps in my career,' she said, in a carefully rehearsed speech.

I stared at her. 'Would those next steps happen to be in the direction of Wilderstein PR?' I demanded. 'Am I going to be reading it in the next bulletin of *Patsy's News?*'

Yaz's deeply scarlet cheeks told me everything I needed to know, and she just nodded her head.

That was also her last day in the office, but not because I escorted her out (I couldn't do that until I had proof she had signed up to my competition), but because that night Yaz apparently suffered a catastrophic health crisis. She developed a mouth ulcer.

'I need to see my doctor ASAP today,' she wrote in an email I received at seven o'clock the next morning.

Soon another email arrived, this time from her dad, who said that he and her mum were worried sick about her. 'Yaz is much iller than she is letting on and will need a minimum of another two weeks off. This is not how she imagined finishing up at Queen Bee but unfortunately she will not be able to make it back in there because her doctor will not allow it.'

Had Yaz's mouth ulcer become so inflamed that she could no longer speak for herself? Had she also lost control of her hands, which meant that she could now no longer write an email? What other twenty-four-year-old gets their parents to write their sick notes? This was just hurtful because Yaz was someone whom I had nurtured from the start.

A few days later I wrote back to Yaz requesting her presence in the office to prepare with the handover for the Bee who would be replacing her. After this, Yaz, who had miraculously regained control of those hands of hers despite her illness, typed yet another email advising me that she'd sought legal advice and since she was entitled to ten sick days a year, it was definitely sayonara. She would do the handover, over the phone, from the couch at home. No, wait – the hospital. So much for loyalty. Was this the same Yaz who had pleaded with me for a job despite never finishing her course? The same Yaz who had basically offered to work for nothing if only we would give her a job? Not that I had ever taken her up on that freebie; I was definitely not into exploitation of labour. A courier was dispatched to pick up her thousand-dollar BlackBerry Z10 handset, pronto (all Bees had the best mobile technology because part of their job was to Instagram, tweet and Facebook the shit out of every event we put on and every new product to hit the showroom).

That night when Michael and I were in bed, I told him the story of Yaz and how Queen Bee was unravelling fast.

'Look, Jazz, why don't you sell the agency now while you can still get a good price for it and just do nothing but organise the wedding and look after Fifi and me? You know I have enough money for all of us.'

'I'm sorry, Michael, but I can't,' I said softly. 'I haven't worked hard my whole life just to let it all go like that. I won't be defeated by Diane Wilderstein and a pile of dodgy Russians.' The idea had only appealed to me when Ivan and Svetlana had seemed kosher and because I had arranged to still be involved in my business as a consultant.

'It's not about saving face, it's about our life together,' Michael replied quietly.

🍸

They say that you have to bottom out before you can even contemplate climbing up again, and it was certainly true in my case. Each day took on a new rhythm of resignations from either clients or staff, who, despite their denials, were always heading to the same place – Wilderstein Public Relations. And besides the fact that it was all so bleeding obvious, I had to wait to read about it in a daily bulletin from *Patsy's News*.

Patsy herself (aka Fabian Tarrington aka Fabs, a onetime event supremo who was well and truly plugged in when it came to hearing all about public relations accounts in Sydney) called me a couple of times to try to arrange a coffee meeting.

'You know, it's been so long since we've seen each other and I can't wait for you to update me on all things Fifi,' cooed the reed-thin blonde over the phone. But of course I knew that the real reason she was ringing me was so she could report how I was coping with my agency disintegrating around me.

'I can't wait to see you,' I lied, 'but Queen Bee is operating at full speed at the moment as we prepare for a top-secret launch involving a US star.'

That made Fabs' ears pick up. 'Oh, really?' she said. 'I thought Tod Spelsen's launch went over to Wilderstein PR.' Oh right, thanks for that. When they were handing out lessons in diplomacy, Fabs was too busy having her hair extensions weaved in to read the memo. She had to be the most insensitive person in the industry. Only the celebrated columnist Pamela Stone could be more devastating, but at least Pamela knew when she was being bitchy. Fabs rarely did, she just said the first thing that came into her head.

'Fabian, I think you'll find that the star Queen Bee is launching in Australia is just a tad bigger than Tod Spelsen, who is just a schmutter cutter after all.' I was stretching the truth a bit here because, when it came to the fashion industry, Tod Spelsen was neck and neck with Chelsea Ware. But by the time we had finished promoting her, this would not be the case – at least in Australia.

'Now you've got me excited,' said Fabs. 'Are you sure I can't write anything about it today, just a little line somewhere?'

'Nope, sorry – that would spoil the surprise,' I said. 'But I promise to give you an exclusive the moment they're in the air.'

Sure, I could promise her an exclusive on my part, but I planned to have Chelsea papped the moment she arrived at LAX en route to Sydney, along with a leaked story about the big launch; at the same time I would swear to Fabs that it hadn't come from me. I could hardly control what happened with regard to the international media, could I?

One person who couldn't hold back was Wally Grimes, who was having an orgasm each day I lost another client. Just a few days ago he posed the question that the charity event I was working on was one to raise some much-needed funds for my household. I never react to Grimes' poisonous diatribes but this time I just couldn't help myself. The words 'vicious', 'bitter and twisted' along with 'badgering' featured prominently, as well as a clear direction to look in the mirror, if he could manage to focus after all the bottles of free champagne he had sunk at lunch. As text messages go, it was something of a masterpiece but I shouldn't have reacted at all because he was the newsprint equivalent of a troll. And you should never feed the trolls or give them any oxygen at all.

What did I tell you about everything having to bottom out before it got better?

It suddenly got a lot better at the Queen Bee office following one of the most bleak lunch hours in our short history. With both accounts and staff turning their back on the agency, the remaining Bees and I gathered around the conference table to eat a meal of stale Ryvitas with Vegemite and left-over Boca Lupo's drinks from our last jeans' launch, and at the same time to try to work out a plan of action. It was quite fitting the only drink left for me was grapefruit-flavoured, because I already had a bitter taste in my mouth from all that had been going on.

But then, just after lunch, I had a call from Marshall Coutts, our lawyer. 'Jasmine, remember when we advised you not to have any business dealings with Ivan Shavalik?' he said excitedly as soon as I had picked up the phone. As if I could forget.

'Yes,' I said simply.

'Well, our information is that he has thirty days to stat dec on why he shouldn't be deported, and in the meantime he's banned from having any business dealings in Australia at all.'

OMG, I haven't felt this excited since the new season of Balmain accessories landed at Cosmopolitan Shoes in Double Bay and Rose gave me first dibs on them. I'd tried to play nice with Ivan by hooking him up with Diane but the two of them had formed an alliance against me, which I definitely should have seen coming. Now I just basically wanted him and Svetlana to mosey on back to Moscow and leave Sydney's PR landscape safe and secure.

'That's great, Marshall,' I said at last. 'But it's my under-standing that he's currently backing the Diane Wilderstein PR company and has signed on as her business partner. So, what will that mean for that cosy little mutual-support group?'

'Well, put it this way,' said Marshall, 'he better not have put anything in writing or transferred money into any banks associated with Wilderstein. Not only would this be against the law and may result in all of her accounts being frozen while both the Immigration and Taxation Departments take their time to follow the paper trail, but they could both also face prosecution for money laundering.'

It was a lot to take in, but an image immediately popped into my head of Diane Wilderstein, fag hanging from the corner of her mouth, standing over a sink filled with bubbles and with newly washed notes pegged on a line. I started to laugh out loud.

News travels exceptionally fast in our industry, and you don't have to be a psychic to feel the sudden surge of electricity in the air. As the news of Diane and Ivan's predicament percolated through the bitchy public relations industry faster than a turbo-charged espresso machine, suddenly Queen Bee's phones started ringing all at once. The most honest of our clients informed us they had made a terrible mistake in moving to Wilderstein PR and asked if we could look after them again. Of course we took most of them back on, but we raised our fees by twenty percent. We weren't so gracious with some of our old staff members, who a few weeks earlier couldn't wait to move on to work with my nemesis. We had already started a massive recruitment drive through Power Brokers, one of the smartest new agencies, who were handpicking staff they guaranteed would be tomorrow's leaders. I didn't worry about that so much – I knew I could mould anyone who was savvy enough to realise that PR was not just about air-kissing and giving out goodie bags.

Besides, I had other things on my mind – like flying to LA to pick up my wedding gown and organising my new client Chelsea Ware's CD launch in Sydney. Michael had been amazingly sweet about the return trip to LA, possibly because it involved our wedding. He had not only asked his mum to stay over and look after Fifi along with Anna for the best part of the week that I would be away, but he had also paid for three first-class seats on Qantas – for myself, Shelley and the wedding gown, because it was far too precious to try to stuff into a suitcase (unless I was in the habit of travelling with a Louis Vuitton steamer trunk. Perhaps that would come later).

The morning of our departure was typically frenetic. I wanted to spend as much one-on-one time with Fifi as possible, and there were loads of last-minute arrangements to put in place for Chelsea's arrival. We had organised a press reception on the afternoon of day one in order to accommodate all the requests for interviews; Chelsea would have just a few hours to get over her jet lag before hair and makeup arrived to sort her out. The following day she was booked on all the breakfast TV shows, featuring a live broadcast of her performing her single from Martin Place. The actual launch party would take place the following night and, in between, Chelsea and her minders wanted to pack in as much of Sydney as possible before she was left to her own devices later in the week. Very kindly, our high-profile financier mate, Don Dell, had offered us his magnificent yacht *Basket Case* to ferry her around the harbour in style.

In the end, with the phones in the office running hot, Shelley and I almost missed our flight. Although we were both excited about the trip, I wasted too much of the first-class luxuries out cold in my skybed; then again, sleeping is one of the greatest luxuries around.

Y

Getting through LAX is never easy – even from the pointy end of the plane, which gives you special passes and a really good headstart on everyone else. Still, by seven thirty we were checked into The Peninsula and I was tucking into my usual breakfast of poached eggs, a slice of smoked salmon and one piece of toast.

We felt so fortified by this that Shelley and I were waiting outside on the pavement for Vera Wang to open up, and thankfully my gown was ready and waiting for me, just as beautiful as I remembered it. A dozen shots on your mobile phone cannot capture the beauty and mystery of a wedding gown. Seeing it, Shelley was on the verge of tears again. I had my final fitting, and the seamstress told us the dress would be ready for collection the following day.

'Come on, we have to celebrate,' said Shelley. 'I don't care what else you think you have to do – your immediate task is to drive us to the Polo Lounge. We're having Dom and oysters.'

The Polo Lounge at the Beverly Hills Hotel is one of those places in LA where you're guaranteed to see at least one celebrity if you wait long enough. Maybe the fact it's almost inaccessible to paps in the hotel where some of the world's biggest stars – including Marilyn Monroe and Elizabeth Taylor – have cavorted that makes the Polo Lounge so special. It's almost a living shrine to old-school Hollywood glamour. (The appeal definitely isn't about the food, which is, at best, average.)

Shelley worked her magic and we were shown to one of the A-list booths facing the courtyard. At an adjacent table sat an elderly couple in head-to-toe white who were treated with so much reverence by the staff that you would have thought they owned the hotel. Shelley and I tried not to stare but we had never before seen a woman in a white tracksuit with a real diamond tiara on her head. It was an entirely different approach to sport luxe, but probably not one that was destined to catch on.

'Here's to you, Jazzy Lou,' said Shelley, raising her glass of Dom. 'May your marriage be everything you want.'

I toasted to that too, wishing that Michael and Fifi were here with us, but it's bad luck for the groom to hang around when you're buying the dress.

We took another sip of Dom. The bottle must have set Shelley back at least six hundred dollars, but as usual she insisted she was not being extravagant. 'How many times will you get married, Jazz?' she said, topping up my glass and nearly giving the over-attentive waiter a conniption as he tried to sprint back to our banquette to do it himself. (He needn't have worried, we were always going to give him a big tip – after all, we want to return to the Polo Lounge.)

She went on immediately, 'No, don't answer that – just once, right? Michael is pretty spesh and you don't wanna change baby daddies on Fifi anytime soon. And anyway, the guy would have to be an absolute saint to be more patient and accommodating than Michael.'

I laughed at the thought: besides Michael, the only thing I found deeply seductive at the moment was my bed – the sight of it meant that I got to recline for at least a few hours.

Both of our heads flicked around at once as we saw a familiar figure stride into the Polo Lounge as if he was taking a stroll down Woolloomooloo wharf during a packed lunchtime.

Russell Crowe, wearing a backpack and looking straight ahead with grim determination, was about to walk right past our booth with a couple of middle-aged men who looked as though they worked in the film industry. Since he purposefully wasn't making eye contact with anyone, I shook my head at Shelley, who seemed hell bent on attracting his attention. If she wasn't wedged into the booth beside me, I swear she would have bounced up and ran after him because the way she was waving (fruitlessly, I might add) to him suggested that they were old buddies. Russell's body language alone made it very clear that he was a human no-fly zone. As Shelley leapt about behind the table, like the cheerleader from hell, I watched as he and his group made their way out to the garden terrace and sat with their backs to the window.

'Maybe I should send over a bottle of Dom,' suggested Shelley, already looking around for our hapless waiter to do her bidding.

'No, no, no!' I insisted, as the server almost skidded to a stop in front of us.

'Did you need something, ma'am?' he enquired hopefully.

'Yes,' I replied, swinging my leg at Shelley under the table. 'May we have another bottle of sparkling mineral water?'

'What did you do that for?' asked Shelley, rubbing her leg, when the waiter had walked away.

'Just to save you from making a fool of yourself when Russell refuses to accept your champagne or, maybe, takes it and doesn't say thank you. How pathetic are we going to look then?' Russell Crowe was just as unpredictable as any actor at the top of their game. The only thing for sure when it came to possible reactions from Russell is that he detested people who wanted to fawn all over him. And, after all, who could blame him? Russell Crowe is nobody's performing seal.

'Wait, really?' she said doubtfully, as the waiter returned with our mineral water.

The problem with Shelley was that she could already visualise the Instagram shot of her and Russell Crowe cheering each other with the flutes of Dom. A shot like that would potentially bring in hundreds of followers. Shelley was particularly competitive when it came to social media, and wanted to be the queen of it among her tight circle of friends. She already had one advantage over them – she bought thousands of dollars worth of designer clothes on a regular basis and always found creative ways of shooting them next to their special bags or the Net-a-Porter packaging. She made them look so lustworthy, she could have worked in window dressing for Louis Vuitton.

Now we both watched as another waiter, no doubt the most senior in the Polo Lounge, delivered some cocktails and a beer to Russell's group. Rusty was drinking the beer. Dom Pérignon? That was strictly for sissies.

In the absence of having her mug captured on Instagram next to Russell's, Shelley set about filtering some shots she had taken of other wedding gowns at Vera Wang. That was what she had been doing while I was in the change room, Instagramming the shit out of everything.

As I looked at some of the gowns she had focused on, it suddenly hit me – I had no shoes!! Or rather, I had around forty pairs of designer heels at home but none of them suitable to wear with a thirty-thousand-dollar Vera Wang customised gown.

'OMG, what the hell am I going to wear for shoes?' I cried, so loudly that a very stylish woman who happened to be walking past our table glanced down at my feet. She probably expected to see me still in a pair of towelling pedi slippers or something.

Shelley almost choked on her champagne. 'I knew we'd forgotten something but I couldn't think what it was!' she exclaimed. 'And there's nothing I like more than shopping for shoes, unless it's finding the right handbag to go with them, which thankfully you won't need because you will be carrying a bunch of flowers.'

Never had a bottle of Dom and a chef's salad and oysters been consumed so quickly, but Shelley still insisted on picking up the tab and tossed a couple of the sesame-seed-covered grissini into her Birkin for later. She had immediately understood that the quest for the right wedding shoe would be so consuming that eating again might not fit into the schedule anytime soon.

In the end we split up just as we hit Rodeo Drive; Shelley went to Barneys and Saks while I went off to Christian Louboutin and Prada. For the first half hour we texted pictures of possible shoes to each other before I found the perfect pair of Louboutins that weren't on display but were instore, with limited sizes left – luckily this included my size. They had my name written all over them.

'Shelley, I've found them. Come meet me at Louboutin,' I hollered into the phone. 'And I just had a text, the dress is ready to pick up as well.' (I guess there hadn't been much to do and it was a slow day there.)

When we finally made it back to Vera Wang, with Shelley juggling the three pairs of shoes she had found along the way while she was looking for mine (for her to return empty-handed from a trip to LA was nothing short of sacrilege), our next problem was that my wedding gown didn't fit in the hired car – or rather it did fit in but it meant there was no room left in the vehicle for Shelley and me – so we had the store ring The Peninsula to have the hotel's Rolls sent around to pick it up.

Just getting the gown up to my suite at The Pensinsula was a major production, with two porters employed in delivering it. Only when it was hanging safely in its own cupboard did I turn around and notice that lying on the table was a package from Sprinkle, the Beverly Hills cupcake outlet that had people queuing up outside. Inside were enough beautifully created cakes to throw a first birthday party for Fifi – but who had sent them? Most of my friends were aware that I had a sweet tooth but that I would do almost anything to avoid temptation.

A pristine white card was perched beneath the ribbon, embossed with the letters TS – for Tod Spelsen. Let me know if you're available for tea, it read. We have so much to discuss. A quick check with Lulu revealed that Tod had been calling the office and she had let him know I was in town and at The Peninsula. But what kind of a fashion designer sent women cupcakes? Perhaps he was branching into a plus size collection. Or perhaps he just thought that flowers had been done to death.

12

Tod Spelsen had been left with egg on his face. And not just any old oeuf but a freshly barn laid, supersized variety fit for a branch of Ralphs in Beverly Hills.

The Australian designer had been in the hunt for another sort of egg – some glistening beads of the finest Sevruga caviar in downtown Moscow. It was a taste of the good life that would have come with his promised status as a superstar designer in eastern Europe. As everyone knew, when it came to spending, Russians were the new Arabs.

But now all those 'big in Siberia' promises had left him slightly shattered after the news had filtered out that Ivan Shavalik and the seriously unchic Diane Wilderstein's partnership had fallen apart. Worse, Shavalik had accrued huge debts and was set to be thrown out of Australia. So Tod Spelsen's dream of effortless world domination – and especially the chance of being big in Russia – had been too good to be true after all.

With his launch into Australia and New Zealand now heading rapidly towards countdown mode, Spelsen was desperate to hook up with the public relations agency which always delivered the goods, fast. Queen Bee had this reputation because I would always pull an all-nighter or do whatever it took to get the job done. Of course it was delicious that Tod Spelsen was now knocking on Queen Bee's doors begging to be let back in, but our primary duty was to successfully launch reality star Chelsea Ware's first CD in Australia.

The timing of it all was so tight – even though the wedding dress expedition had gone off without a hitch, we were due to leave LA in a few days before Chelsea so everything could be organised for her arrival. On the other hand, I never like to let anyone down – particularly a prestige brand like Tod Spelsen which had the potential to make us a key player in international markets, allowing us to launch even more big brands in Australia, where everyone from Zara to Top Shop was trying to colonise. Another plus with Tod's label is that we would have every one of Sydney's tribe of serious, full-of-themselves fashionistas trying to gain access to him, so we could maybe get them to look at some of our lesser known labels along the way. Tod would be our PR bargaining chip of the year.

You see, it didn't just come down to money. Tod's budget would probably come in somewhere under Chelsea Ware's, but while Chelsea would give us a bit more cred when it came to celebrity, promoting Tod's high-end beauty line meant that we would be taken more seriously in the marketplace. Soon after discovering the cupcakes, I received a call on my phone from Tod's assistant, the dreaded Jenna Katz, who was so cold on the phone she would make the perfect door bitch at Pelicano. Despite the fact they now needed me, her voice still as icy as the Russian tundra. 'Tod will see you at his office tomorrow at five pm,' she informed me, sounding as if she couldn't quite understand why I had been granted this special audience with him.

She was about to hang up on me, no doubt thinking it was mission accomplished, when I said breezily, 'Sorry, that won't work for me.'

Seconds passed. I could almost hear Jenna hyperventilating over the phone. For a moment I thought she was about to have a fit. Should I call 911?

'What?' she said finally, as if she hadn't heard me correctly.

'Yeah, no, I can't make it,' I said, deliberately sounding as Aussie as possible, just to drive her a little more cray-cray. Of course, this was extremely childish of me but I'd had to grovel to her in the past and had been rejected, so I did indulge myself with a little play acting since the roles did seem to have been reversed a tad. Besides, right now my intuition told me that if I pretended to be quite blasé about the whole deal, Tod was going to be even more desperate to sign on the dotted line.

'I'll be heading back to Australia soon with Chelsea Ware to help her launch her CD there and I'm afraid that this is seriously eating into my time in LA,' I explained, feeling a little sorry for Jenna, who clearly wasn't used to the man she idolised being turned down by anyone – let alone an Australian PR lass. I pressed on regardless. 'In fact, the only time I could see Tod is around five o'clock today here at my hotel. Oh, and do thank him for the fabulous cupcakes. They were delicious.'

What sounded as if it might be a massive fault on the line was actually just Jenna sucking in her breath. 'You can't seriously imagine–' she began, but I cut her off at the pass.

'Sorry, Jenna, love to chat but I have to take a call from Australia,' I lied. 'Maybe we can all catch up next time?' And with that I hung up with a great big smirk on my face. This was shaping up to be the best trip to LA ever.

I had already half decided that perhaps I could do an early breakfast meeting with Tod the next day, but I wanted to make Jenna work for that. All of her skills as a personal assistant who knew how to wangle a meeting would be called into question – and I wasn't even a big-name celeb but just a lowly publicist from Sydney.

Now it was all about Instagramming some shots of the Sprinkle cupcake gift to my hundred thousand followers on that social network. (More people followed me than picked up a copy of *Mode* to read every month, but that was because I worked it.) I wondered whether it would be too OTT to snap Tod's handwritten note as well? Perhaps I'd just show a little bit of it, leaving off his signature. If people really wanted to know who had sent them, they would have to do their detective work.

QueenBeePR – Nice receiving this very delicious gift of #Sprinklecupcakes at my #Peninsula hotel suite today. The personal handwritten note was a sweet touch #designertalent #AussieinLA #Aussiewood, I posted. Surely that would get them all talking – and dear old Fabian, who followed me with missionary zeal on Instagram, would be beside herself.

It had already been a huge day but there was just enough time left to go over the final details of Chelsea Ware's arrival and media commitments in Sydney. Eric, her agent, had been emailing his amendments to the schedule all day. It turned out that due to some late filming commitments Chelsea would be flying into Sydney a couple of days later than we planned. But at least it gave us lots of time when I was back on the ground to get the paps prepped for her eventual arrival and to put some more arrangements in place. Unfortunately, Eric wouldn't be able to make it down with her on this trip himself but he was sending along his loyal, brilliantly unassuming assistant, Louise. I was thankful about this. Louise would be Chelsea's human buffer zone and official porter. She would be the one who would keep the reality star on track for all her appointments, no doubt saving me the trouble of hauling Chelsea's arse out of Sydney's best clubs so she could look all fresh for her early morning interviews. At least, I hoped that's what the plan would be. I'd had enough of a tough time a couple of years earlier with Raven, another American pop starlet, who had hit Sydney as the pin-up girl for Vixenary lingerie but then spent most of her time in Kit and Kaboodle's toilets barely able to keep her knickers on. Raven was only in

Sydney for a few days but she'd managed to get around like the town bike – and one with a scooter motor.

Y

'I think I'm going to have to go out and buy another suitcase,' Shelley announced as she walked into the sitting room of our Peninsula suite, her arms loaded with various garment bags but her sights set on the fast-diminishing tray of cupcakes.

'Red velvet!' she cried, as she put down the garment bags and twirled a cupcake theatrically towards her mouth, licking her lips lasciviously. 'Mmm, my favourite.' Momentarily satisfied, she returned to her predicament. 'I don't know how I'm going to fit this lot into my luggage.'

Somewhere in between trying to track down the perfect wedding shoe for me, Shelley had managed to clean up on Rodeo Drive. No doubt she'd been in too much of a rush to try anything on (she thought she was only slightly bigger than an LA size zero). Even I struggled to fit into her purchases most of the time, and I was rail thin, having been blessed with the Formula 1 of metabolisms – plus I never seem to be able to sit down long enough to finish a plate.

'Uh-uh, you're not going to take over one of my bags,' I warned her as I noticed her eyeing off my largest suitcase, which looked invitingly empty. But this was only because I hadn't started to pack it yet.

With Shelley happily heading off on yet another shopping expedition on the pretext of needing to find a bigger suitcase (she absolutely hated exercise but when it came to shopping,

she suddenly found the stamina that was almost Olympian),
I went through my emails again. Most were from Lulu advising
me about which clients wanted Queen Bee to look after them
again following the apparent demise of Diane Wilderstein's
business. There was a grim missive by a certain oily male
publicist, Sam Hevner, who was urgently tracking down some
of his client's tennis gear which had been sent to the Queen Bee
office by mistake after it had been used on a special celebrity
tennis day we had organised for one of our soft-drink clients.
The only problem was that it had been sent several months
ago, and when no one came to pick it up the gear had been
earmarked to go to charity. Now Sam was furious, claiming
that if it was not immediately returned we would be charged
the full price of all the garments and sued by their client.
This was ridiculous: it was simply not our responsibility to
sort out another PR company's delivery issues. Eventually Lulu
had been able to track down most of the garments but Sam
wasn't pleased that he'd have to send a courier to pick them
up. This petty-mindedness was undoubtedly one of the reasons
why the Sam Hevner agency has remained so small. Plus the
fact that Hevner had been so sleazy in his prime that he had
basically hit on everyone with a pulse.

Meanwhile my buddy, Luke Jefferson, wanted to interview
me about Queen Bee's dealings with the Russians. But it was
far too early to go into the ins and outs of why our deal had
fallen through – besides, when it came to Diane Wilderstein,
anything could still happen.

I had hardly noticed how much time had passed when I received a call from reception. Answering quite casually, I thought it would probably be someone wanting to know when they could clean the room or return the laundry. I almost dropped the receiver when the front desk informed me that I had a visitor downstairs – a Mr Tod Spelsen. 'Shit!' I yelled before I could stop myself. 'Tell him I'll be right down.'

Probably the last thing I had expected was that Tod would obey my directive to meet at my hotel. At the back of my mind I had been gearing myself up for another call from poor Jenna Katz, insisting I hotfoot it to Tod's headquarters first thing in the morning. But to actually have him come to me was beyond what I had thought possible.

And what the hell was I wearing? It should have been something by Tod himself, but I was wearing my favourite outfit of skinny jeans, a Balenciaga tee, Balmain blazer and Alaïa heels. There really wasn't time to change, so I just scooped up my iPad and keyboard, threw it into a Chanel pouch and headed out the door.

Tod was sitting with his back to me as I walked into The Peninsula's drawing room, and this time his dark curls had been contained in a ponytail so prissy looking it would have put Karl Lagerfeld's to shame. But there was nothing superior about the look on Tod's face when he turned and saw me. He looked embarrassed that he'd had to come to me cap in hand.

'I've already ordered tea for two,' he said after I lowered myself into a chair opposite him. 'This hotel has some of the rare Da Hong Pao tea available at the moment and I couldn't pass it up.'

Fortunately I had heard of Da Hong Pao tea, having read about it in some airline magazine (it was said to be the most expensive blend of Chinese tea in the world), but I wasn't about to admit to Tod Spelsen that this was as close as I had got to it. I would have to watch him to see whether the correct etiquette was to take it straight.

'We seem to have had a missed communication,' he said, adjusting the sleeve of what looked suspiciously like a Gucci leather jacket. Tod didn't yet design his own collection for men, but surely it could only be a matter of time.

I nodded – best not to say too much at this point, just let him do the talking. I had very early learnt the value of silence: it made most people feel uncomfortable and they would rush to say anything to fill in the space. It was a power play.

'Look, I stuffed up,' he suddenly blurted out. 'I really liked all of your suggestions for our launch back home but I'm afraid that I had to give the account to Wilderstein PR because it was going to be our gateway into Russia.'

I was taken aback. Before now I had encountered cool Tod, gushy Tod and businesslike Tod, but this celebrated designer contritely admitting to me that he had taken the wrong path was completely unexpected.

I glanced at his face and noticed he was making full eye contact with me, no doubt confident that once he gave anyone his undivided attention, whatever he wanted was pretty much a done deal. And I had to admit I was hardly immune. I was

almost having an out-of-body experience. Here was Tod
Spelsen, one of the world's hottest fashion designers, sitting
across from me at The Peninsula Hotel in LA, begging me to
take his account. I wouldn't dare come up with a scenario like
that in my dreams in case I was laughed at by the sleep fairy.

I found myself nodding, almost as though my body had
broken away from my brain and was making all the decisions for itself. After all, I admired his candour; it was very
Australian of him to come clean and explain his actions when
most people in the US would never admit to fucking up. I did
want to help him, but it was still going to take some doing
because: a) I was already committed to Chelsea Ware's CD
launch; b) I had Fifi, whom I was missing like mad, to look
after; and c) there was that smallish project of my forthcoming
wedding to plan – with all this work I was definitely not
giving myself enough time to be a bridezilla.

I noticed that Tod was taking something out of his Louis
Vuitton Keepall. He handled the tissue-wrapped box as delicately as if it contained pieces of fine china.

'This is part of the beauty collection we'll be launching
worldwide in just a few weeks,' he said, handing over the box.
'I've selected the products which would be best for your skin
and your colouring and I'd like you to try them. But it's not
for public consumption,' he cautioned. 'Now, about the launch
itself – I wanted the setting to say Sydney, because we are
going to video it and link it to other international launches.
What do you think of having it at the Opera House?'

Absolute nightmare, was what I really thought. The Sydney Opera House is not the sort of place you cruise into at the last moment – it's one of the most in-demand buildings in Sydney. And, besides, Lulu and I had already come up with an astonishing venue. It just didn't seem like the perfect moment to push him on it. More to placate him than anything else, I found myself saying, 'Brilliant. I'll see if I can work something out, although the Opera House is pretty booked out except for some sections of the forecourt which unfortunately do attract a lot of wind.'

Nearly an hour and several cups of Da Hong Pao tea later, we had come up with a plan, one I knew would be a masterstroke in itself because basically I sold him on my original idea but let him think that he had come up with most of it himself. Clutching my Spelsen swag – the beauty products that Tod wanted me to try – I headed back to my room, which now resembled one of the shops on West Hollywood's hippest shopping boulevard, with all Shelley's recent purchases stacked up. Shelley herself was slumped in an armchair staring warily at it. I shared her concern. She probably wouldn't be able to get it all into her bags and out the door without a team of sherpas to help her along. In fact, we needed two sherpa teams because we still had to figure out a way of transporting the wedding dress through US Security and onto the plane. We'd realised it was going to be a logistical nightmare when we hadn't even been able to get it in the car.

I had such an information overload from my meeting that I couldn't even face reviewing all her new purchases with her and making the appropriate squeals of joy. 'I'm beat,' I announced to Shelley and the world in general. 'Let's go get something to eat and tackle the packing and the plotting later.'

Shelley almost leapt from her chair at the suggestion. 'I'm starving, the only thing I've had to eat since breakfast are all those Sprinkle cupcakes – and quite frankly, if I eat another one of those I'll puke. I think I'm over-Sprinkled.' Of course, Shelley clearly had food amnesia. She had conveniently forgotten about breakfast and about our oyster spread at the Polo Lounge where she had singlehandedly dismantled the bread basket, but I wasn't about to take her through it all again.

'There's only one place for it – let's head to Cecconi's.'

Y

Cecconi's in West Hollywood is that rarest of destinations, a hot spot that is actually nurturing. Just the place for Shelley and me to unwind after yet another epic day in LA. The shimmer of Cecconi's fairy lights outside and the odd glint of a camera lens as the paparazzi lay in wait out the front was enough to make me feel a bit reckless, a little excited by the possibilities of what lay ahead. Not to mention receiving a case of the rubber neck from always spinning around to see who or what had just come in. Simon Cowell is a regular here and if he came in tonight with his baby mamma, Lauren Silverman, well my visit to Cecconi's would be a highlight of the year. And if I could somehow get an Instagram of me with the couple – boom! Gossip column heaven. No wonder all the stars love Cecconi's – it's infused with a golden light that makes everyone look as though they're up to that stage post-facial where your skin is glowing and dewy.

'Unfortunately we haven't booked,' I said in my best Australian drawl to the woman who was perched at a little stand by the door. 'We just flew in a couple of hours ago, put our bags down and said, "Stone the crows, let's have dinner at Cecconi's."'

Shelley pummelled me on the back, almost shrieking with laughter, but I pretended not to notice. The Aussie accent and the news that you have just flown in is guaranteed to open some doors in LA. And there's no such thing as being too OTT Aussie – not when you have Sam Worthington and Hugh Jackman running around banging it on as if they had just stepped off the set of The Man from Snowy Bloody River or something.

'Certainly, ladies. Welcome to Cecconi's. Please come this way,' she beckoned for us to enter and delivered us to yet another stunning looking server, who led us to a table, which was luckily in eye view of the bar and the entrance. Before Shelley could even think of plonking herself down on the more 'scenic' of the two seats, I'd already taken it and accepted a menu.

'I don't know what to have,' said Shelley, her eyes sparkling as she watched a waiter grate some fresh truffle over a plate of steaming risotto at the next table where a glammed up couple were ostentatiously holding hands. They didn't look familiar but I'd have to covertly peer at them through my reading glasses to know for sure. Shelley, bless her, wasn't taking any notice of them at all, she only had eyes for the pasta, weighed down with scampi and crab which the amorous couple was also being served.

'I think I'm having pasta for an entree and a main,' Shell announced. 'Unless you order pasta too and we share?' she suggested hopefully.

But I just smiled and shook my head. I hadn't even succumbed to pasta when I was pregnant and had an excuse for having a rounded belly, so I certainly wouldn't be going there now. 'Don't forget all those designer clothes you bought, Shell,' I cautioned. 'Spanx can help but they can't work miracles. Maybe a salad to start?'

With a large glass of Californian wine each and a lull in the number of people coming through the door, we should have had time to talk about the wedding, but now there were much more pressing issues for me – like trying to fit Tod Spelsen's launch into Queen Bee's schedule. 'And he also wants us to organise a massive fireworks display,' I told Shelley, 'because everyone knows that Sydney Harbour is famous for its New Year's Eve fireworks.'

'Don't you think he would be happy with a few sparklers?' she asked, twirling the grissini in her hand like a fiery wand.

'Signora?' One of Cecconi's Italian waiters immediately appeared, thinking that she had summoned him. Shelley immediately took the opportunity to ask for two more glasses of wine; she works on the premise that you should never waste an opportunity to get a waiter to fetch something for you.

The place was heating up as a parade of girls who looked like Victoria's Secret models arrived toting oversized handbags and, almost knocking the bread stick out of Shelley's hand as they glided past. Carrying an extreme handbag was very LA. Who knew what the hell they had in there. The bag du jour – the Céline Trapeze – could easily accommodate an entire wardrobe of LA mini dresses.

'Oh my God,' laughed Shelley. 'Those girls should need licences to carry those ginormous things. They're lethal weapons. Haven't they discovered the clutch yet?'

Never mind that we had capacious matching Birkins sitting beside us. We were tourists and on a mission – which reminded me, my call to the office was seriously overdue. Even though Cecconi's was noisy, I had to find out what was going on.

Lulu answered on the first ring. Before she'd even said hello, I started alerting her to the plans for Tod Spelsen's launch and then asked how everything was progressing for Chelsea Ware's arrival. The way things were going we would have to find a platoon of new staff.

'So what else has been happening?' I asked her finally.

'Sooo much,' said Lulu breathlessly. 'The phone hasn't stopped ringing with old clients and prospective clients. Meanwhile the word is that Diane Wilderstein has upped sticks and moved to Bali.'

'What?!' I screamed so loudly that Shelley almost choked on her wine. She looked at me inquiringly. 'The dreaded Diane has supposedly fled Sydney,' I hissed across the table, not really believing for a second that the old dragon would give up that easily. She probably took a long weekend in Bali to put everyone off the scent as she tried to regroup. You could never write off Diane Wilderstein – not when I was still around. It seemed as though her main mission in life was to try to bring me down, especially now that I had bequeathed her a dodgy business partner. But, hell, it had really put her name up in lights again. She should have thanked me instead of trying to kidnap all my clients.

Just then, a familiar figure walked past us. OMFG, it was Dr David Gruber, plastic surgeon to the stars, resplendent in head-to-toe Dolce & Gabbana, which made him look far older than his fifty years. He actually resembled a walking comic strip.

Famed for his exquisitely maintained eyebrows and extremely full lips, Dr Gruber's other signature was his latest-model Bentley, navy blue with cream upholstery. It was a familiar sight going through the McDonald's drive-thrus – because the good doctor, who'd had his stomach stapled in a bid to lose weight, could not shake his burger addiction. Although according to TMZ, the only order he made these days was for a Filet-O-Fish burger, because it was coated in mayo and slipped down easily.

On previous trips to LA I'd had a few consultations with him to get some Botox, and we'd got along so famously that on my last consultation, which was on a Friday evening, he'd invited me home to have Shabbat dinner – the traditional Friday night Jewish meal – with his family.

'Hello, Dr Gruber,' I yelled above the din at Cecconi's.

He stopped dead in his tracks, and the bony blonde he had been following through to a more private room did a pirouette and came scampering back to his side. From memory, Dr Gruber's wife Vivienne was dark and curvy – still, you never knew what miracles could have happened in LA in just a few months.

Dr Gruber was staring at me now, one eyebrow cocked so theatrically in the air that I was worried about it coming down again. It appeared as though all of his features were on a ten-second delay.

'Shalom. It's me, Jasmine Lewis,' I reminded him. 'Remember, you invited me to your home in Bel Air for Shabbat dinner after our consult?'

'Of course,' he said smoothly and leant in for the kiss, while urgently signalling to his scrawny companion to go on to their table.

'And this is my good friend, Shelley Shapiro,' I continued. 'We're both on a flying visit from Sydney.'

Dr Gruber looked as perturbed as his facial muscles allowed. 'And you didn't call me for an appointment?'

Were my frown lines that pronounced? It was all Diane Wilderstein's fault, and the Russians. It was a wonder I hadn't aged at least ten years since I'd had Fifi. I wondered if I would have time for a quick consult tomorrow. It was probably the last time I would be in LA before the wedding.

'Funny you should say that,' I said, grinning at him. 'Got anything around nine tomorrow?' I looked at Shelley, who was kicking me under the table. 'Make that a double appointment.'

Dr Gruber consulted his iPhone. He looked doubtful, but was also obviously a little uneasy about being seen out with a blonde by a patient who had met his wife.

'I'll see if I can move something around,' he promised, glancing in the direction the blonde had disappeared in. 'Call me at eight.'

'You didn't have to kick me under the table,' I assured Shelley as our meals finally arrived with a drop-dead-gorgeous Italian waiter who almost made Shelley forget about hers – a miracle.

I Instagrammed a photo of my grilled bass fillet, which was so perfectly presented it almost belonged to a Hermès window display for a fishing expedition on Lake Como, then I tweeted up a line about Cecconi's, linked in a mention of Dr Gruber (but not his companion), and finally turned my attention to my iPad, which was sitting next to me in my Birkin. Social media can be a bitch sometimes. A quick glance at my emails: Lulu had already responded to our phone chat by giving me more detail on exactly what was going down at Queen Bee.

Hi Jazzy,

Great to talk and you sounded so happy and relaxed. Now where do I start? As I mentioned, the phone has been ringing off the hook with clients wanting to rejoin the agency. I told them you would get back to them in a couple of days.

You remember how we were asked to donate several crates of L'Eau sparkling water to that fashion designer,

Claire Green's, brand anniversary party? Of course, we agreed only if we could get lots of celebrity shots through. Well, unfortunately all the shots we got back showed the sparkly crew clutching Aqua Vert water. Claire herself had this big, cheesy grin on her face and was holding up a bottle of Aqua Vert like it was a trophy. We've asked for our water to be couriered back pronto or we'll bill them.

I groaned. Since when was bottled water such a precious commodity that hosts had to find a water sponsor as well as every other bloody kind of sponsor for their events? It was all getting just a little ridiculous.

'Bad news?' asked Shelley.

'No, just the usual petty stuff going on over us supplying bottled water for that designer Claire Green's party – but it was nowhere to be seen in the shots.'

'I never liked her,' responded Shelley. 'And her clothes – well, really, not my cup of tea.'

Well, that's it then: Australia's most determined shopper had spoken.

Shelley and I really did need that team of sherpas to help us check out of the hotel and check into LAX. My Vera Wang wedding gown seemed to take up more room in the town car than both of us and our bags combined because it couldn't be crushed. Thank heavens for the porter and for the Qantas first-class check-in who managed to get us processed through US customs in double quick time – even when the gown threatened to get stuck inside the hand luggage x-ray machine.

'Have you just got married, ma'am?' asked the operator suspiciously, looking hard at Shelley. WTF?

'No,' I replied, willing the gown to come through unscathed. What if security decided to cut it up to see if we were carrying drugs? I could just imagine myself taking it back to Vera Wang and asking them to fix it or re-create it. Or if it did make it through intact, would Florida in Double Bay be able to remove any possible grease stains from the inside of an American Customs office?

Luckily the gown came through pristine and, less than an hour later, Shelley and I were on the plane exploring our first-class cabins and sinking a couple of glasses of Dom.

It was fortunate that Chelsea Ware had delayed her trip because it allowed us both to relax on the flight home.

'Jazzy,' said Shelley, who had emerged from the bathroom in her Qantas pyjamas and already signalled for another two glasses of Dom, 'let's get this party started.'

The problem with the overnight flight from LA to Sydney is that there is a small margin of time to sink a few glasses of champagne and sample Neil Perry's first-class menu to really get your money's worth of the outrageously expensive ticket before you have to start preparing yourself to hit the ground running at the other end.

Shelley and I could always amuse ourselves in the air, but she became even more outrageous if there was a gay flight attendant or two to egg her on. She almost never disembarked from a plane without a 'goodie bag', which would include some vintage champagne carefully wrapped in the airline's finest linen napkins with some expensive chocolates thrown in as well. Around Shelley even the bitchiest queens were transformed into Jewish mothers organising a care package just to ensure she wouldn't die of thirst between the time she stepped onto the air bridge and when she arrived at her final destination.

It happened again on this flight when I put an end to the drinking and asked for my bed to be made up. Shelley was disappointed but continued to sip her drink when the lights were turned off. Even with my B80 earphones on I could hear the clink of the bottle against her flute as she topped it up.

All I could think about now that we were finally heading home was how happy I was going to be to see Fifi and Michael again. I had missed my young daughter so much – when I wasn't with her it sometimes felt that her birth was something I had dreamt up and, as for Michael, well how lucky was this girl to find such a hot, understanding man. As we flew closer to Sydney, I prayed there wouldn't be any delays because I couldn't wait to see them on the other side of customs. Michael had promised me that he would be there and he was bringing the G63 so that he could fit us and all our bags in, plus the driver and car just to transport the dress (as there was no way we could all fit – even if the G63 was an eastern suburbs upmarket version of a tank!).

13

Sydney dines out on salaciousness. Gossip spreads faster here than Justin Hemmes in a new Aston Martin. People just can't get enough of it, especially when it's about someone who's obscenely rich, successful, trashy or larger than life (bless you, Belle Single, for ticking three out of four boxes). Alas, I fitted two myself (not trashy – how dare you!). I'm wealthy and successful but, as a publicist, I believe in flying under the radar. I'm only there to enhance my clients' reputations, not to enjoy myself at their expense. So don't expect to see me dressed up to the nines, swanning around at one of Queen Bee's events. When I'm working, I am everywhere and nowhere – you will never see me preening on the red carpet. In spite of this, I soon discovered there was a group of people who were out to get me – and no, not just the usual suspects. They shared the following characteristics: a sense of entitlement, an aversion to working hard, and greed. They thought that all it took to enjoy the trappings of success was just to be around it. It didn't seem to dawn on them that you had to pull long hours and show true dedication to make it happen. The other thing they had in common, of course, was that they had all passed through the doors of the Queen Bee agency and not exactly enjoyed a happy landing. Can there be anything as potentially fatal as sacked staffers out to exact their revenge?

There were around five staffers who had been relieved of their posts since Queen Bee had been formed. It was probably about the same level of staff attrition as many other companies in the media, but when you are dealing with young girls who want to be celebrities themselves, the bruises to their egos can sometimes be painfully inflated. I was soon to discover that at least three of them had joined forces to shoot me down as if I was one of those sideshow targets at the Royal Easter Show. Step right up, Jazzy Lou just became fair game. But remember that old cliché, when the going gets tough . . . ? Well, in my case, the tough become twice as effective.

Gossip spreads so fast in Sydney you can almost see its trajectory from email recipient to mobile phone number before it continues to go buzzing around offices, cafes and launch parties. It positively pulsates in Divorcee Heights – those waterfront apartment blocks in Darling Point, home to the savvy second wives who are all 'resting' between very expensive 'engagements'. (Only suitors bringing forth Cartier, Bvlgari or something very large, sparkling and hand-crafted from the Jewellery Concierge should think of trying to scale Divorcee Heights.) No wonder these women have so much time on their hands to spread slander.

You can sense gossip's vibration. It has its own force field of electricity – almost a power surge before it finally reaches the person who was the subject of it all. Then all the communication lines spring into life at once, and the person's inbox instantly becomes fuller than Ajay Rochester's bikini. This is the tipoff that life has suddenly taken a very twisted turn.

Barely was I back in the office after LA when some of the newest Bees out in the main office seemed to become almost dizzy with excitement as they held their phone receivers up to their ears. I noticed them all glancing at me and whispering, but I thought they were just planning my top-secret hen's party. I didn't comprehend I had suddenly become a victim of gossip until Lulu walked into my office, her face white as a sheet. So much colour had drained from her cheeks that she looked as though she'd walked straight off the runway from a Romance Was Born show. She was clutching her BlackBerry as if it was contaminated. Poor Lulu's hands were trembling so much she could hardly carry the device; she looked like Clarence, the alcoholic waiter who had recently been fired from uber-fashionable watering hole The Vineyard.

'Jazzy, you really have to hear this,' she said apologetically. 'Someone has been leaving horrible messages about you on everyone's mobile phone.' She went on, speaking so rapidly that the words ran into each other. 'None of us can work out whose voice it is but the message sounds really creepy, as if the caller is putting on a false accent.'

My stomach did a neat backflip, as it always did when I found myself in trouble. Usually it was because I was guilty, but this time I really didn't have a clue what I had done. For a moment or two I stared at Lulu without really looking at her – so powerful was the emotion, I felt like I'd just dropped from the height of Centrepoint Tower without stopping at the mezzanine.

What was going on? Was it the Russians again, threatening to sue, or worse? 'What is it, Lu?' I asked.

'Are you ready to listen? It really is quite strange.' She sounded a little bit hoarse herself as her hand hovered over the 'play' button.

'Go for it.'

The voice that filled the room was spoken in an irritating whisper which grated and also sounded familiar, but I couldn't place it.

'This is a message for anyone who has ever had dealings with Jasmine Lewis, owner and operator of the Queen Bee Agency,' it began. 'This woman believes that slave labour is acceptable. Anyone who works for her will be subjected to pure torture. I should know, I've been there. Day in and day out I would march myself into the Queen Bee office knowing that at some point during the day, I would be brought to the brink of tears, or to a point where punching a wall seemed like a good idea. You might have called me a "Slave to Fashion".'

The caller then went on about the other ways that I had apparently made her life hell. She even mentioned the food which was banned from the showroom at lunchtime. And she was right; greasy food was out because I didn't want to risk our high-end samples being marked. I also didn't want anything to go out to the magazines reeking of eau de trans fats. Honestly, do you blame me?

There were also some caustic comments about my Bees having to work around the clock. Well, welcome to the world of PR. My staff did have to pull late nights at some of our launches. And who wouldn't want to be at one of the hottest tickets in town? They would be pissed if they weren't there.

The message was apparently being sent out to stop anyone else from foolishly wanting to work for me. 'I hope this serves as a warning to all young publicists: Do not work for Jasmine Lewis. There's a reason the staff turnover rate is as high as Snoop Dogg. And it's also why it's so bloody easy to get an internship there. When you walk into the office everyone looks like they're ready to evacuate and not go back.'

Fan-bloody-tastic – what was Queen Bee, a feeder station to Lifeline? Apparently, making my staff almost suicidal wasn't the worst of it. In fact, according to the person who had donated this bile to the answer phones of Sydney, the atmosphere was so toxic at Queen Bee headquarters that the Environmental Protection Agency regularly sent out a squad of men in breathing apparatus to ensure the noxious fumes didn't travel far. The entire PR company was deemed to be an environmental health risk.

I was also accused of having callously stolen Michael from Belle Single, who truth be told gets through men just slightly quicker than it takes her nails to dry. Belle, bless her, has always operated on the principle that she's not going to look young and sexy forever so she might as well make the most of it while she can. And she's also a firm believer that you have to kiss an awful lot of frogs before you get to your prince; so the faster you get through all of them, the sooner you'll find happiness. Michael was probably already so far down on her list of former boyfriends that she could scarcely recall having dated him.

I glanced at Lulu, who was so embarrassed at having to bring this sordid message to my attention that she could barely look at me.

'It's okay,' I reassured her. 'Just make sure that no calls are put through to me till I work out a strategy for dealing with this.'

My stomach was feeling as queasy as if I had sent out for a chicken sanger from one of our local cafes in Alexandria, Salmonella Central. The place was actually a godsend when I had to lose the last six kilos following Fifi's birth – I lost most of it following just one takeout order. There was almost nothing safe to eat there – even the Vegemite toast might be smeared with a knife which had cut through rancid butter. Strangely, Salmonella Central was not yet on the government's name-and-shame list, probably because the local health inspectors had their work cut out for them in this semi-industrial area.

It was just as well I decided to go silent, because soon everyone from gossip diva Luke Jefferson to Bernard Mealy, the head of *News at Eight* (the TV station where I was a regular guest on the morning show *Breakfast of Champions*) was trying to get through to me for comment. I wondered whether Diane Wilderstein was somehow behind it, but it wasn't her style to take so much trouble. While she was certainly manipulative, for her it was all about instant gratification. Diane was so lazy she often didn't turn up to her own clients' events but dispatched minions to run them (such as me when I worked for her). Diane might have been co-opted into Toxic Message-gate, but she wouldn't have been the mastermind. So who was the one who had started it all? The name Kelly Young kept coming to me from some of my contacts who had been helping get to the bottom of it.

Kelly Young, a former staffer, definitely had an axe and a half to grind with me because she was now the focus of a criminal investigation, brought on by yours truly. It all started after Kelly, whom I'd taken on at Queen Bee shortly after her arrival from California, came to me one day looking teary. She had to return home because her dad was ill. What to do? Kelly had been one of the most diligent of Bees. The clients loved her and so did the editors of some of the glossies, who admired her style. Funny how a warm and sunny American accent can compensate for what we discovered was a seriously compromised set of morals.

After Kelly told me her story, Lulu and I came up with the idea that Kelly could open a branch of the Queen Bee agency in San Francisco. We already had four clients who were based there and we were sure she could get more. So, armed with the company credit card and some powerful computer equipment, Kelly went home to 'Frisco', and for a while all went well.

But then Kelly was suddenly hard to find.

This didn't make sense to me as I stayed up late at night, working to ensure she had everything she needed at the start of her business day. Meanwhile I was eagerly awaiting responses to some of my queries. I kept wondering why I was unable to reach the person who was on my payroll.

Then came the whisper that Kelly Young was working for Agosta and Lil, the internet store some fashionistas here were starting to become addicted to for distinctive dressing. I didn't believe it but called their office anyway – and was put straight through to my employee, who was currently pulling a nine-to-five wage there.

. It was eleven o'clock at night here when I found her out but I had a lawyer's letter sent out to her by seven the following morning, advising that her access to all Queen Bee' emails and networks had been severed. In the days that followed, the credit card company sent me a list of purchases made on the company credit card, from Banana Republic, Jeffrey Campbell Shoes.com, One Love Studios Ltd, LA Bond Inc, LuisaViaRoma.com, and Vintage Wheels – the last to the tune of twelve thousand dollars.

Of course, it was all classified by the credit card company as financial crime, and as such I wasn't liable to pay them. But it caused Kelly some massive problems, including the possibility of being charged with theft if she ever set foot on Australian soil again.

If what my underground sources told me was true, this could be one of the reasons why she was now trying to have her revenge. Even more worrying, Kelly had kept in touch with some of the old Bees who had left the company in less than pleasant circumstances. The more I thought about it, the more certain I was that it had to have been a group effort timed to upstage my wedding and the rebuilding of the agency.

Unfortunately, there was only one way to find out for sure who was behind this poisonous diatribe and that was to call in the lawyers and get them to track down the phone number. But first of all we had to ensure that none of the media organisations printed the contents of the call or, worse, put the audio on their websites. We needed to send them all a lawyer's letter threatening defamation. Lulu was already one step ahead of me, and she had the call transcribed and recorded, ready to be sent out to Marshall Coutts.

So while half of the city was salivating over my perceived fall from grace, the other half – who had gleefully hit the button marked 'Forward' on this toxic recording – were suddenly in the position of having passed on information which had the potential to land them in a courtroom charged with defamation.

𝛾

It took approximately ninety minutes to deal with the sordid residue of gossip, and then it was on to the next item on the jam packed schedule: putting the finishing touches on Chelsea's CD launch party.

The brief was to find a location that said old Hollywood glamour, and my clever Bees had managed to secure the rooftop of one of Sydney's oldest and most gracious apartment blocks, the Atlas in Macquarie Street.

'Tell me again how we managed to persuade the Atlas's managing board to allow us to do this?' I asked Lulu, still puzzled as to how she had pulled it off. You would usually have as much success with securing that space as you would in holding a Peter Alexander pyjama collection launch in the crypt of St Mary's Cathedral. It was pretty much sacrilege.

Lulu beamed at me and I noticed for the first time she was looking a little bit rock star in her Alexander Wang maxi-dress teamed with the Givenchy ankle boots which she could wear for hours at a time without seemingly getting sore, when everyone else only wore their investment shoes from Cosmopolitan in Double Bay when we were being visited at the office by bona fide celebs.

'Easy,' she said. 'You know the socialite Juliet Bassett-De Plassy — the former Paris runway model who married that French banker, Maurice De Plassy, who eventually left her for her best friend's daughter?'

I nodded. It had been the lead item in Pamela's column for two weeks. People couldn't get enough of it. And when Juliet and her BFF, Belinda, showed up for Sunday lunch together at Catalina, there was almost a traffic jam on New South Head Road as word spread among the eastern suburbs social tribes.

Some of those who had been seriously gossip-deprived tried to get a table at Catalina just so they could gawp, analyse the body language and try to listen in. Luckily, Belinda's daughter didn't join her mother and Juliet for lunch or there would have been pandemonium.

'Of course. Who could forget that spectacular divorce, which threatened to turn into a criminal trial because the girl was only fifteen years old when they met?' I said. Breaking that juicy story had been one of Pamela's best coups ever. In fact, if they gave Walkley Awards to gossip columnists, Pammy would have scooped the pool that year with the tale of betrayal, lust and forbidden sex.

'But he swore they didn't sleep together until she was eighteen,' Lulu added helpfully. 'And you know Juliet got the huge Atlas apartment in the settlement, but now he's trying to prise her out of it, offering her less money than it's worth. She wants to have the launch party on the roof using his name so that he won't be at all popular with the Atlas's board and they won't be keen to have him back. The scandal of having a noisy launch party at the Atlas would be all too much: by the time they finish with him, he won't want to know about his place.'

'Fantastic, Lulu,' I said, thinking that with my number one Bee, at last I had someone prepared to go even further than me when it came to putting together the right event for our clients.

This party was going to be gorgeous – the Atlas's rooftop reeks of old Hollywood grandeur but with a backdrop of the Sydney Opera House and the lush, velvety green of the Botanic Gardens. The images would go right around the world. I could almost envisage them on the opening page of the *Daily Mail* website.

But its success would also come down to the guest list. We definitely had to bring the A-list, not the desperadoes who wanted to be seen out at all costs.

'Who do we have?' I asked Lulu, taking the list from her. 'And why does Raelene Bax have a question mark next to her? Isn't Josh in town as well? Surely he could make an appearance. After all, he's one of Chelsea's mates?'

Raelene and her fiancé, the actor Josh Sweetwood, had not yet set a wedding date but Raelene was already thinking big. Despite the fact that under her own steam she only released a capsule collection of knits once a year (she was too busy travelling on set with Josh the rest of the time), she had already employed her own 'manager' to look after her social engagements. Or had she? As I've mentioned, the mysterious Sharon had never been sighted or spoken to but was flat out issuing badly written emails to publicists, magazine editors and TV producers, laying down the law on her requirements for Raelene's personal appearances. In her emails – which sounded eerily similar to the way Raelene spoke – Sharon insisted that Raelene could only be assisted by the top makeup artists and hairdressers, and that only the most exclusive European labels could be sourced for her to wear. She was the full on publicist's nightmare. In complete contrast to this regal and difficult mindset, Josh was the all-Australian bloke who had found international success partly because he always played up his down-home charm.

'So what's Raelene's issue with attending Chelsea's launch?' I asked. Surely Josh and Chelsea got along famously from hanging out in West Hollywood. They had been photographed in the same group of celebs, attending a birthday party for Hollywood producer Nad Coleman at Sur. Raelene had been there as well and had seemed to be very happy in Chelsea's company.

'No, that's not the issue,' Lulu responded. 'Sharon is demanding that Raelene and Josh are only snapped for the social pages of *Harper's Bazaar* and not for the daily or Sunday papers.'

'That's ridiculous,' I snorted. 'We need all that publicity now, not when the magazines come out in three months' time. And if they're serious about it I'll have to get an extra security detail just to keep the photographers away from Raelene and Josh. We'd have to smuggle them in and out of the event, which would defeat the purpose of having them there in the first place. Who else has confirmed they'll be there?'

'Three former Miss Universe Australias, that complete nutter Lillian Richard–' began Lulu, reciting the list in her best singsong voice.

'Do you think we should offer Lillian a free blowdry by Leonard at her office?' I interrupted. Lillian was the editor of *Eve Pascal* magazine. 'All that hair of hers blowing free and wild on the roof as she bears down on Chelsea could scare the crap out of her. It could even be an accident risk if it got caught on one of the props. And Lillian always looked so much more elegant in an up do.'

'Copy,' said Lulu. 'Lillian has already put in a request for Chelsea to appear nude on her magazine cover, artfully shot of course.'

'Of course. Having a nude celeb on the cover is her go-to initiative when she has no other ideas. Who else do we have?'

'Allison Palmer, Samantha Priest, Tom Reynolds, gorgeous Dalia Goodman who is in town to film an Australian Tourism commercial and may bring some of her celebrity mates with her, but we don't know their names yet. Then there's the dreaded Matt Ashley, the A-grade cricketer who's a chance to surpass Warnie.'

'Of course,' I agreed. 'But we also need some really big names besides the local television fodder. And we must have someone to run the red carpet – I don't want all those tragic models thinking they own it.'

Queen Bee had been the first agency in Sydney to instigate a red carpet bitch for our events. We needed someone strong at this event, because some of the more relentless partygoers out there had absolutely no shame. Fortunately, Susie Solomon had just returned to town from LA where she worked for a film company helping to organise film premieres, and she was ruthless about who she would and wouldn't let onto a red carpet.

Everything seemed to be falling into place.

14

In this town personal trainers think they're the new soapie stars. No, scrap that, they think they're Leonardo DiCaprio fresh off the set of *The Great Gatsby*. TV stars are far too low down in the food chain for them.

I should have been trying to spend my spare time catching up on my sleep and playing with Fifi but, since I had so much stress in my working life (ah yes, that would be the Russians, the vile phone messages, Chelsea's CD launch and, of course, Tod Spelsen's beauty launch), I seriously needed a serotonin boost and to firm up a little more before the wedding. But with Noah, my Israeli personal trainer on vacay in Tel Aviv, who to go with? The last thing I needed right now was to put my back out.

Lulu saw John Warren-Smith but in a group class, and the reports weren't encouraging. He sounded as though he had a bigger ego than Seal's.

'He's driving me crazy,' Lulu complained. 'His "Six Weeks to Sublime" boot camp is the Hollywood fitness regime from hell. All those solarium sessions of his must be melting his brain.'

'Come on, Lulu, it can't be that bad,' I said, studying her slender frame. Lulu did have a good appetite, especially when the Cupcake Queen came to call, but you would be hard pressed locating her tummy. Maybe she had a tiny one hidden under her armpits?

'You wouldn't believe it. I've spent gruelling Saturday mornings running on the soft sand at Bondi at quarter to six and doing hill sprints up to St James Park but he doesn't pay any attention to my specific body issues at all. He just regards our boot camps as an opportunity for him to flirt with the prettiest girls in the group and not us fatties who need to do the most work.'

'Fatties?' I spluttered. 'Seriously, if you think you're fat, what hope is there for the rest of us?'

'Look, if he "helps" Lizzie out with her hamstrings by stretching her into a compromising position one more time, then I might throw a kettle bell at him. While you were away, I was following his strict no-carbs/paleo diet – the meat, veggie and no-fun diet – when I received a little update in my inbox at Monday lunchtime. Yes, just while I was tucking into my chicken salad – hold the oil, hold the mayo, hold the avo, and defs hold the flavour – up pops a picture of Jessica Alba's arse and a reminder to watch what I eat at lunch. That was on top of the end of winter email warning me not to ruin my training by stuffing something bad in my face during the last of the cold snap. Honestly, it made me want to dive into a vat of chocolate fudge then and there.'

Okay, so John Warren-Smith was definitely out, because the last thing I needed was a food Nazi stalking me as well as all the other weirdos.

Shelley wasn't having much more joy with her PT, yet another celebrity trainer, Shane Pongrass, whose claim to fame was that he'd had three training sessions with Megan Gale before she relocated interstate. Shelley was really peed off because Shane had made her do burpees for being five minutes late. She'd waged war with him via email over this, threatening to leave, but by all accounts he won because he had attitude right up the wazoo.

Shell, this discussion is really boring me, began one of his emails back to her when she had complained about being punished for turning up late (after all, she was the one who was penalised for having to pay him the same amount whether she was early on late). *The rules are simple. You're late, you do the burpees. You carry on about it and refuse to do them, you go and train somewhere else. Two rules, it's an easy equation. The fact that we now have over ten emails about this is pissing me off enough as it is. Either turn up tomorrow morning for your training with the right attitude, or don't turn up.*

Of course Shelley packed it in. Who wouldn't? The thing about having a trainer is that you want them to be a partner with you in your health and fitness, not some power crazy, retarded former sports teacher who wants to make you pay for subordination. But Shell did not give in without a fight. She wanted a refund on the money she had already paid upfront. And she got it, eventually.

I sure didn't have the time or the energy to fight with any trainer, so I resorted to the tried and trusted old-fashioned method. I did it myself.

Those early-morning runs where I pounded the leafy and reliably safe streets of Bellevue Hill not only toned up my body but cleared my head as well. I now knew precisely how to proceed with all the different 'challenges' in my life.

Y

Of all the areas that the Queen Bee agency has to be concerned about during a launch party, schlepping our signature goodie bags to the event should not be one of them. It was up to the production company we'd hired to manage the areas that required brute strength. And it was a production company, not dial a male model, so it shouldn't be beneath them to sort out the show bags which weighed a ton. (The male model call-in would come later when we needed to hire some handsome men to escort Chelsea into the event. Nothing like an out-of-work male model to pull that off. We'd been thinking of asking the reality cast of *Bondi Rescue* to accompany her but that would be way too *Baywatch* cheesy. Chelsea was a little more classy than that, as befits the star of *The Bel Air Life*.)

For her CD launch we were giving all guests Byron Bay Cookies, Ice-Watch timepieces, Spanx Skinny Britches, copies of *Eve Pascal* and *Eve Pascal Home*, bottles of Belvedere vodka and shot glasses, plus an invitation to take the latest Peugeot RCZ for a weekend. On top of that there were chocolates, coconut water, Curtis Collection makeup, a selection of ModelCo tanning products and Slim Secrets Fibre Bars. All up, each bag weighed ten kilos, and there were three hundred and sixty of them. We couldn't expect the Bees – average weight fifty kilos or under – to carry them in to the event.

Unfortunately, Jason – the event manager from the production company – wanted all the bags unloaded a couple of floors below the event, which meant the Bees would not only have to carry them up but also to hand them out as guests departed. Yeah, cheers, Jason – we love putting our whole team onto something that your blokes could easily sort out. The goodie bags needed to be left where the Bees could easily access them and then handed over to each guest. No can do, he insisted.

Well, then we will have to employ another company, I bluffed. I hoped he wouldn't twig that it was far too late for that.

It took another twenty minutes of back and forth before Jason grudgingly agreed to send some of his staff to assist the Bees with the bags.

The other 'debate' was with Chelsea's management, who wanted her to wear an American label to the event even though under the Queen Bee contract she was required to wear an Australian designer because she was launching the label on Australian soil. Finally we came to a compromise: she would wear a glittering Allison Palmer gown for her arrival and then change into Christopher Kane to belt out one of the singles from the CD during the second half of proceedings. The American number was chic and elegant, but I was hoping that once Chelsea saw how good she looked in the Allison Palmer she wouldn't want to take it off.

All the rest of the details of the night were working well. There was even more of a buzz about Chelsea now that the leaked photos we had of her leaving LAX had made nearly all the top gossip sites and featured in Luke's column in *The Sun*, netting us a handy fee. Australian chef Michael Moore, who often tours in the States thanks to his top-selling cookbook *Blood Sugar* (suitable for diabetics), had created a cute cocktail menu of Bel Air blinis, Haute hot dogs, popcorn chicken and, to finish, some red velvet cupcakes with stars and stripes icing. We also had Bel Air martinis, champagne and Budweiser.

Anya, Alice and Lulu were in charge of greeting the guests downstairs, while I went upstairs in search of our mysterious hostess, Juliet. Tripping warily between the couches and coffee tables which had been delivered, I finally saw her standing at the end of the terrace looking out towards the Opera House. At first I didn't notice what she was wearing, but when she turned around in the Christian Dior overskirt with sequined hot pants underneath, I was stunned.

'Oh my God, Juliet, I saw that in the window of the boutique a few weeks ago and wondered who would wear it,' I gushed. Actually when I had seen the ensemble in the window what I had really thought was that it was only good for the runway, forgetting that a true eccentric like Juliet could pull off anything.

'Really,' she responded, looking slightly unfocused, her long blonde hair blowing almost on end as if she had suffered an electric shock. She seemed distracted, as if she weren't completely present. Was it the glass of champagne in her hand?

For a split second, I worried that she might be using our event to stage a spectacular suicide attempt. After all, the railing behind her didn't look like it would present much of an obstacle if someone was intent on jumping. Should I dispatch a security guard to shadow Juliet, just in case? After all, she was known for her attention-seeking behaviour, including the time she organised camels to stand outside Chiswick Gardens for her husband's Moroccan-themed sixty-fifth birthday party. Juliet had one camel saddled up for her and trotted around as the guests arrived, not really believing what they were seeing. The bill for the pooper-scooper alone that night had cost more than the birthday cake for a hundred guests from Sweet Art.

'I bought this gown on my last trip to Paris,' she said suddenly.

'Oh, of course. Well, it's so good of you to allow us to hold a launch party here,' I said. 'Please let me know if there's anything you would like us to do to keep everyone happy.'

She smiled wickedly. 'To tell you the truth, the more noise and commotion the better.'

'Well, bump-out is at nine pm,' I reminded her, 'so hopefully it won't disturb the other residents too much.'

'That's okay. Most of them are away at the moment anyway,' she said, lying through her teeth.

I could have stayed chatting to Juliet all night – she was the supreme reservoir of Sydney's old-school social secrets – but I had to tear myself away to get changed. Tonight I was actually making an exception to my usual working gear of jeans and trainers and was slipping into a Roland Mouret with a pair of Christian Louboutin heels which I wouldn't keep on a minute after I had to. This extra effort was for the benefit of the Americans, who were more conservative than us Aussies and expected me to look high powered and glamorous – a fashion authority.

'Jazzy, is it okay for us to send a car to collect Sean Harris, the designer from Lally Is A Star label, his publicist wants to know?' said Lulu over the walkie-talkie, sounding apologetic.

She was kidding, right? 'Oh puhleese, what's his problem, hasn't he got enough money to call a cab? No way will we send a car. Who does Sean think he is, Carla Zampatti? And let me tell you something else, Carla would never ask if one wasn't offered.'

'Copy!' replied Lulu, who thought she was Madonna in those headphones we used with the two-way radio.

Dear oh dear, what was going on with guests wanting to be feted from the moment they left their doorsteps? That kind of treatment was only reserved for true social lions like Carla, the grande dame of fashion. After all, it wasn't as though Lally Is A Star was a major player in Australian fashion – it was very niche. And the only reason Sean was on the list at all was that he and his co-designer were colourful. They were like the clown prince and queen of Australian fashion.

'But wait, there's more.' Lulu was back on the two-way again. 'He wants to bring an entourage with him, including his boyfriend, Ross, and two underground filmmakers who are making a fashion documentary.' She started to giggle. 'They've also stipulated that it has to be a stretch limo.'

'Um, that would be a no. He can only bring Ross, and they can catch a bus for all I care. Or walk, it would probably do them both good,' I said, heading into the small room we had put aside where I could get changed. Sean probably had only a few more seasons left in him before everyone decided they didn't want to look as though they were modelling for their fashion design friend's graduating parade. And then he'd probably have to take a crash course in tailoring and finding ways to enhance the feminine shape.

It wouldn't take long for Chelsea to travel to the event, since she was staying in celeb bolthole the InterContinental, just a few hundred metres up the road. Chelsea's minders, including Eric Lacey, who had been able to come with her at the eleventh hour, had tried to book the Australia suite for her with its dining table and epic views but, since this event was already way over budget and the hotel did not offer a reduction, she settled on a perfectly acceptable executive suite a few floors below. Her rider – the list of refreshment requirements that all big stars have when they step out – was something else again and very California hipster. It included Vichy water, coconut water, goji berries, acai gelato in the freezer, and a small field of wheat grass with a presser. We also decided to leave a platter of Violet Crumble bars, Tim Tams, lamingtons and Anzac cookies in the suite and were surprised when the request came through to have this replenished after just a few hours. All the other requested snacks and drinks would remain untried for the duration of her stay. But more about that later.

Chelsea would not be leaving the InterCon until most of the guests had turned up at the launch. For now, many celebs seemed to be hogging the red carpet. Some celebs just will not move off the photo wall until every angle has been exhausted.

When I saw stylist Justin Lee in his rust-coloured velveteen jacket, cheesy bow tie, 2009 Calibre shirt with the black trim around the collar, shiny black trousers and fake Gucci loafers, I wanted to call the fashion police. He had definitely committed a crime against sartorial style. Never mind that Lee, who worked as a stylist for a chain of suburban fashion malls and had his own radio spot on a western Sydney station, was preening himself on the red carpet as if he was Tom Ford. Maybe he thought everyone loved him for his retro fashion moment, but he just looked as if he hadn't been able to borrow anything decent. How he got past Susie Solomon, I don't know. Maybe it was because he was one of the first to arrive. Only a couple of photographers (one who worked for Froth – a suburban newspaper with a small readership – and the other a ring-in from a photo agency) were obediently snapping him. Both of them probably shouldn't have been in the camera area anyway but we'd wanted a big mob of photographers so Chelsea would feel more at home. Behind Justin I could see a queue of real celebrities forming for their moment on the photo wall, and I heard Susie's familiar voice urging the lesser-known people to walk on through.

'Just go right into the party and get yourselves a drink, guys,' she said to the fabulous nobodies. 'And have a great night.' Susie always tried to sound upbeat and friendly, because you never knew when the nobodies might become the faces du jour.

I couldn't help myself: I marched right up to Justin, almost knocking him over in mid-preen. He would never become the next face du jour – more likely just another pain in the rear. 'Please, Justin,' I said firmly, 'we have to keep it moving.'

Justin glared at me for a moment before quickly composing himself. He probably realised that if he carried on the way he was going, his invitations to Queen Bee launches would dry up faster than Warwick Capper's acting roles.

'Sorry, Jazz. What can I tell you, they just wouldn't let me walk on,' he said, winking at the lensmen, who had now well and truly put down their cameras and were chatting between themselves. (This is what snappers do when they want to make a pointed statement to someone they can't stand or whom they find boring. And if they really detest a celebrity – usually because the celeb has committed the number one sin of refusing to be photographed with a new partner or when there is a fresh news angle – then as well as putting down their cameras they will perform the ultimate snub of turning their backs.)

Before Justin disappeared to the furthest reaches of the rooftop, he tried valiantly to be cool. 'Oh my goodness, Jazzy, don't you look stunning tonight,' he said, giving me a wet kiss on the cheek. 'I couldn't really see you before with all those lights in my face.' Yeah, right, he wished he had been dazzled by flashguns. 'What's that you're wearing? No, wait, let me guess. Camilla and Marc?'

'Almost,' I replied, smiling grimly. 'It's Roland Mouret.' (What's a few thousand dollars price difference between friends?)

'That was my next guess,' he said, moving away as fast as his fake Gucci loafers would take him and almost lunging at a model waiter carrying a tray of martinis. 'Thanks for inviting me, Jazzy. It certainly has all the hallmarks of one of your best events,' he said over his shoulder as he bolted.

I made a mental note to consign Justin to the social wilderness known as the D List for a few weeks. He was getting off easily. Anyone who dressed as badly as he did and carried on as grandly deserved to be banished.

'Jazzy, Jazzy, can I take your picture?' called out Marco, our favourite paparazzo, armed with his Canon and the ability to sell photos around the world in nanoseconds, often in partnership with Queen Bee.

'Hi, Marco,' I said smiling broadly at him. 'Only when the guest of honour is here.'

In one corner of the rooftop, Cleo Jones – the gorgeous gay model turned DJ who famously only dated actresses or supermodels – was setting up in the booth she had insisted we construct for her in case someone should try to stalk her. Jones had her own celebrity manager and a list of requirements that would probably make even Jay-Z blush. She needed her own lighting guys, some imported designer threads which she reserved the right to keep, bottles of Patrón tequila with lemons, limes and fresh mango juice, some freshly peeled lychees and vegan snacks from Misschu. Despite all that, some of our clients just couldn't get enough of her, so they gladly met all of her demands, including her exorbitant fee. It was probably those shots of Cleo with her tongue down the throat of an American fashion star at the Coachella music festival in Palm Springs which had them so titillated they just had to be around her. They also wanted to boast that they had met her.

I flirtatiously blew Cleo a kiss and shimmied (my dancing is lousy) over to her as if I was already grooving to her sounds. She wiggled her hips back at me sexily.

'Wow, you look so hot tonight, Cleo,' I panted, as if exhausted by the effort. 'Is that a Balmain leather jacket?'

She nodded her platinum-blonde mohawk, looking pleased that it had been noted she was wearing six thousand dollars on her back which she was not paying for. 'I couldn't resist it when I saw it on the stylist's rack,' she said, giving me a hug. 'Hey, I really hope you like the sounds tonight. I've put together something special for our guest of honour, cut with some of her music.'

'Do you know each other?' I asked casually but feeling dread in the pit of my stomach. A lesbian love affair 'down under' was perhaps not an ideal headline for the star of *The Bel Air Life*, but then you never can tell. Really it all should be about the CD and then the reality show.

'No, I just met her once at a party at the Chateau Marmont for Naomi Watts,' Cleo said with a sigh. 'She seems like a really cool chick though.'

'Oh, she really is, Cleo, and once the formalities are finished I am going to bring her right over to hang out with you for a bit.' Which, roughly translated, meant: I am going to do the upmost to ensure that you two never cross paths.

'Perfect,' she said, slipping on her headphones again. Conversation concluded, I had just been dismissed. With Cleo it was always about scoring points.

A familiar-looking couple had just arrived and were being led inside by a nervous-looking Anya. I must have missed the signal from Lulu on the walkie-talkie to pre-warn me about the arrival of Raelene Bax and Josh Sweetwood.

Raelene's 'manager', Sharon, had won the battle about the couple not posing for snaps on the red carpet, and they would be photographed exclusively by *Harper's Bazaar*. A small private booth had been assembled with an ultra-exclusive photo wall and a security guard to deter other guests from trying to crash the booth. But I had my plan B: Marco's brief was all about getting as many candid shots of the couple – preferably with Chelsea – as they could. Of course, it wasn't Raelene that was important, it was Josh.

Evie, a journalist from *Harper's*, was also on site to do a mini interview with the couple, and I couldn't resist going over to see how it was going.

Despite her painful attitude, I had to admit that Raelene totally looked the goods in a fire-engine-red J'Aton gown which showed off her minute waist, while Josh was in a black shirt, black tuxedo jacket and black jeans.

'Thank you for joining us,' I greeted them warmly and kissed them both on the cheek.

'Pleasure, thanks for asking us,' Josh responded. 'What time is Chelsea arriving?'

'Soon,' I responded. 'Probably ten minutes away.' After all, most of the major players were here now, so Lulu could give Chelsea's management the signal to leave the hotel.

Then I noticed Raelene was scowling at me, which made her face look a little bit comical because her Botox meant that the only negative expression she could manage was her lips turning down and a puckering around the side of her nose. Raelene was years away from needing Botox but she claimed it was a preventative measure. I refused to acknowledge her negative attitude and smiled warmly at her in return. 'Sorry, Jasmine,' she said stiffly, 'but we are just being interviewed by Emily and you're interrupting.' I could see Josh blanch at her tone.

'Actually, it's Evie, not Emily,' I said sweetly. 'And I just wanted you to know that in the absence of Sharon I am happy to help out.'

'Sharon?' Josh mouthed at Raelene. Hmm, maybe they hadn't met? He turned back to me. 'Look, we really appreciate your help, thank you so much,' he said.

I stepped back politely so that Evie could continue with her interview, and smiled encouragingly at her.

'So, do you expect to spend more of your time together on location for Josh's new movie in LA?' asked Evie, all angelic blue eyes and soft, fluffy blonde hair. If I wasn't mistaken, that fitted black and cream lace dress she was wearing was by Collette Dinnigan. No wonder Raelene's lips were so tightly pursed. Evie was only around twenty-two years old, and Josh seemed quite taken by her cherubic looks.

Evie tried again. 'So, Josh, tell us about your next film project. Is it true that you've been cast in a Scorsese epic?'

Now it was Josh's turn to look uncomfortable. 'I'm really, really sorry but it hasn't been confirmed yet,' he said.

Evie swallowed hard; this joint interview was proving to be the most difficult of her short career. In the next few minutes, Raelene refused to answer nearly every one of her questions on the grounds they were an invasion of privacy. Even an innocuous question about the direction of her next collection yielded a sharp 'no comment'. It soon became clear that although Raelene wanted her photo to appear in the pages of *Harper's Bazaar*, she didn't want it to be tagged with any more information than her name and the details of what she was wearing.

In desperation, Evie finally said bravely, 'Okay, moving on. Can I ask you the name of your dogs?'

'I would really like to avoid anything to do with my personal life,' Raelene started, hitting her stride with her usual answer.

I had to step in. 'Raelene, I really think you have to give them that one.'

Josh looked relieved and smiled gratefully at me, and I walked quickly away. Raelene, I decided, had dropped a few stitches in her brain and then some.

'Chelsea and her party are on their way up,' Anya said urgently over the two-way radio as I scurried to meet them at the lifts. A group of suave male models in tuxedos were already waiting there to escort her in. Marco had noticed the signal and was right behind me so he could get the precious candid arrival shots that nobody else would have.

Quite magically, just before Chelsea walked onto the terrace, the ubiquitous speakers began to play a track from her CD.

And didn't she look drop dead in her Allison Palmer head-to-toe sequined gold gown.

'Chelsea! Chelsea! Look this way,' the photographers called out the moment they saw her, while Susie Solomon urgently moved everyone else off the red carpet.

'It's so great that you're here,' I whispered to Chelsea. 'And you look sensational. Let me know if there's anyone who takes your eye.'

We were running to a very strict schedule. Chelsea had approximately ten minutes at the photo wall and twenty minutes mingling with guests before Sydney's seasoned Hollywood reporter, Lloyd Jenkins, helped her up onto a small dais to interview her, and then she would slip away to change into her Christopher Kane dress (as we had prearranged) and reappear to lip-sync her single with a band. All that was left to do was the *Harper's* shoot with the backdrop of the Sydney Opera House below her like an enormous sculptural fashion backdrop, and then she would be out of there and on her way to a private dinner at Icebergs Dining Room at Bondi. By the time she was tucking into her exotic entree, many of the guests would be flying so high from all those martinis and champagne they would hardly notice she was gone. Well, that was the plan anyway.

Unbeknown to me, absolute mayhem was about to break out. You see, despite Juliet's advice to the contrary, there were quite a few Atlas residents home on this particular night and they were not at all thrilled by the commotion on the roof.

As I would later discover, Aldo Pavoni, who once owned a chain of menswear boutiques with the hottest labels until he retired from the fashion industry to travel the world (keeping his Atlas apartment as his Sydney pitstop), had at first thought all the equipment being ferried up to the roof was for a magazine shoot. He had happily headed out to dine with a friend at the nearby Rockpool Bar and Grill but was appalled when he returned home to hear what he thought was a rock band on the roof as Chelsea performed her single to a rowdy crowd. After a frenzied ring-around to some of the other Atlas owners who were in town, he decided the most effective way to put an end to the commotion was to cut off the electricity for long enough to send a message to organisers.

Just a few moments before Aldo put his plan into action, Chelsea and Eric had stepped into the lift on their way out to dinner. Lulu was waiting on the ground floor to usher them into their car. But just before the doors closed, Eric discovered he had left his phone behind in the green room.

'You go on down and sit in the car,' he directed Chelsea. 'I'll be right there.'

Cleo was also heading towards the lift after completing her DJ sets and leaving her crew to pack up (she didn't want to look as though she didn't have anything to do either). She greeted Chelsea warmly as she stepped into the lift and pushed the button to take them down the fifteen floors.

Chelsea responded with a cool smile as she didn't recognise Cleo. The ambitious DJ had seen Chelsea once or twice at the Chateau Marmont, and she was planning to remind Chelsea of this before they hit the ground level. But, as it turned out, she had a bit more time to make the TV star's acquaintance than she'd expected, because they had only made it as far as the sixth floor when there was a huge whoosh and all the power went out, leaving the lift stranded somewhere between the fifth and sixth floors.

'Oh my God, we're going to die,' screamed Chelsea, who had been knocked sideways by the sudden, grinding halt. So alarmed was she – believing that a terrorist attack was under way – that Cleo, who was usually hysterical in stressful situations, realised she had to remain calm and in control of the situation.

'It's okay,' she told Chelsea, helping her to regain her balance and giving her a reassuring squeeze. 'The lift has just got stuck. It's fine. I'll call the lift company.' But when she lifted the receiver to her ear the line was dead.

Standing beside the electrical cupboard on the ground floor, Aldo Pavoni heard chaos breaking out all over the building and he quickly flicked the switch on again. Instantly all the lights came back on, including in the elevator. However, the elevator itself remained jammed.

'Won't be long now,' Cleo assured Chelsea, who was crying so hard that her eye makeup had run and she looked like a member of Alice Cooper's backing band.

'I don't think I can breathe,' she cried, clutching at her throat.

'Don't be silly. There's plenty of air in here,' Cleo told her.

And then it happened. Moments after Cleo thought it would be a good idea to give Chelsea a comforting hug, she suddenly started to kiss her on the lips. At first it was soft and gentle, but when the DJ felt the reality star's body almost involuntarily move towards her, it became more passionate, and Cleo found herself thrusting her tongue into Chelsea's mouth, right in through those blindingly white, perfect Californian teeth.

Maybe it was the fact they were trapped together in such a potentially dangerous situation that also served to heighten emotions? In any case, it was at least five minutes before Cleo tried the phone in the lift again, and this time it was answered by an operator from the lift company who assured the women that help was on the way.

Meanwhile, on the other side of the art deco lift doors, all hell was breaking loose as Eric and Lulu were the first to connect the elevator alarm with the fact that Chelsea had failed to materialise from it. Lulu called me immediately on the two-way, and I went to join Eric outside the lift.

'Another woman was walking into it with her just as I stepped out to get my phone,' Eric told me. 'I think it was the girl who was working the DJ booth. We've got to get them out of there. Chelsea suffers from claustrophobia.'

Of all the people to get stuck in a lift with, I thought, the edgy and slightly spiky Cleo wouldn't be my first choice.

Several loud sirens from the street signalled that the fire brigade had arrived. This was later confirmed by Lulu. 'The firies are here. The firies are here!' she yelled into the walkie-talkie, sounding so excited that she could have been introducing the sexy entertainment at Coco Man of the Year. 'Do you copy?' she added, no doubt trying to impress the men in uniform.

'Copy,' I confirmed. 'It's all good in the hood.'

I looked around to find Juliet to ask her about getting the guests down via the fire stairs, but she was nowhere to be seen. I later discovered she had quietly slipped away earlier in the evening so she could play an innocent bystander if the neighbours complained about the noise and the shit hit the fan.

Eric wasn't prepared to wait until help arrived. 'Which way are the stairs?' he panted. 'I gotta get to Chelsea and try to talk to her through the lift doors. She's probably hyperventilating now. And Jasmine,' he added, almost as an afterthought, 'if she suffers in any way, including developing a post-traumatic stress disorder, we'll sue you, do you understand?'

What had happened to the sweet, good natured Eric – he had suddenly morphed into Entourage's Ari Gold at his most lethal. Clearly he didn't handle 'situations' well.

'Copy!' I replied again. 'Loud and clear.' I made a mental note to check out our on-site insurance policy. Surely this kind of contingency was covered – an American guest of honour developing a nervous disorder following what was clearly an act of sabotage? Surely . . .

Fortunately, what Chelsea was suffering from could hardly be classed as a disorder. In the short time before the lift suddenly lurched into life again – thanks to the engineers arriving at the scene – Chelsea and Cleo had discovered they shared such a hot, sexy attraction that they couldn't wait until they had more privacy to explore it. It wasn't Chelsea's first girl-on-girl experience, TMZ had exposed a couple of those in the past but it had usually included some Hollywood hunk joining in as well. This time it was all about the other woman. Those few steamy moments with the tattooed, punky-looking DJ in the lift was the first time this sexual experimentation had moved her on a very deep level.

At first, Lulu thought nothing of the fact that the two young women came staggering out of the recesses of the lift entwined in each other's arms. She just assumed they were helping each other over the trauma of being stuck there for seven minutes and forty seconds.

'Oh my God, I'm so sorry,' she cried when she saw Chelsea's mascara-streaked face. 'Is there anything I can get you? A cognac? A whiskey sour?'

'No, that's fine. But would you please tell the driver there's been a change of plans,' Chelsea began breathlessly, as the two of them piled into the silver Rolls-Royce Phantom which had been parked outside waiting. 'We're both going back to the hotel,' she announced.

Lulu's intuition now told her something was going on even before the words themselves formed in her head. For a moment she was stunned, but just as the driver was about to shut the door, she stuck her head in. 'Shall I tell Maurice @ Icebergs you may be a little late?' she enquired hopefully.

'No, just cancel it altogether.' Lulu heard both women giggling wildly as the car pulled away for the short drive.

A red-faced Eric arrived in the lobby five minutes later, hot and flustered. 'Where is she?' he almost shrieked at Lulu.

'It's okay. Chelsea's fine. She's just returned to the hotel to, um, freshen up.'

'What, by herself?' asked Eric, incredulous.

'No, I believe Cleo the DJ went with her,' Lulu responded diplomatically.

But Eric was hardly listening now. He was dialling her number over and over on his cell phone, swearing when she didn't pick up. Then, without saying anything more to Lulu, he ran off into the night in the direction of the InterContinental.

15

It was another three days before Chelsea Ware and Cleo Jones staggered out of number 1560 at the Hotel InterContinental, slightly tender in certain areas but still deeply in lust. The 'love-in' had been awkward on many different levels for hotel management – not least because the corner suite with views over to the Opera House had been booked by another party. The hotel was forced to give the other guest an upgrade to a much bigger suite and throw in a bottle of French bubbles and a canapé selection to placate them. What else was the hotel's flustered reservations manager to do? There had been no moving the two lovers – they simply could not get enough of each other. In fact, the only time they came up for air was when Cleo had a friend send over some of her clothes and toiletries, plus some of her favourite 'toys' and her laptop.

Her bestie had to leave them all with the wide-eyed bell hop because number 1560 had been declared a no-go zone.

Chelsea briefly got busy calling *The Bel Air Life*'s producers to tell them they would have to introduce Cleo into the scripted reality show because her new partner was returning with her to LA. They would both be there when shooting resumed the following week (good news for the Hotel InterContinental at least – an end was in sight). Cleo had just struck gold, and so had BB Productions, creators of *The Bel Air Life*, who knew a red-hot storyline when they saw one.

Chelsea and Cleo's steamy hook-up in the broken-down lift was all over the gossip sites because, yes, the security camera had been still rolling inside the lift and there was footage, a copy of which I may or may not have had a hand in 'moving on' for an undisclosed sum to a top US gossip site (it pays to be best mates with a certain pap with all the right contacts inside Sydney's most upscale apartment blocks). Chelsea and Cleo's lift episode made Paris Hilton's bloody 'Night In Paris' look like a cartoon, thank you very much. It went viral minutes after it was put up on the site. In fact, I had almost singlehandedly given both of their careers a major shot of adrenalin – strong enough to wake the dead.

'Chelsea's a genius. It's just what the series needed – a lesbian love affair,' gloated Melvin Good, executive producer at BB Productions. 'Do you think she'll try to hold out for more money now? At this rate we could be bigger than fucking *Entourage*. And, by the way, how much is her girlfriend going to want to do this? Has she got a manager we can deal with? Someone's got to put us in touch with her people.'

Unfortunately, managing Cleo Jones was a skill that not many people in Australia had mastered. The problem was that she was super bright and actually knew far more than some of the people she paid to look after her career. She switched agents more often than John Mayer changed girlfriends, which is really saying something. Even I found it tough when it came to trying to achieve the most basic task with her – like booking her for a job. Queen Bee had been let down by Cleo pulling out at the eleventh hour with her signature heap of bizarre excuses. But, luckily, I had discovered her weak spot was flattery and, when it came to receiving it, her appetite was as big as it was for sex. Heavens knows she must have been starved of brownie points as a child – it was the only way you could explain her deep desire to feel appreciated. It never hurt to flirt with her either. (Flirtation with everyone – man, woman, child and even pet dog – was something all my Bees were across.)

Cleo's main problem was an aversion to paying her managers a commission when she felt they had not been on top of their game. Plus she reserved the right to back out of jobs when the mood took her. Her most recent manager, Jon Ford, quit after she had left him in the lurch with a stack of deeply influential beauty executives. Ford had worked hard to land Cleo the role as The Face Of Me, a beauty collection targeted at women who thought they were too cool for the normal brands. Her role was to have been announced at a launch party held at the Ivy with journalists and industry powerbrokers who would all play a role in The Face Of Me's marketing and promotion. No expense had been spared on the event, with Cleo given a Willow ensemble to wear and booked into a suite at the Westin. But, unexpectedly, once she'd had hair and makeup done, she suddenly developed a mystery illness. As the guests were arriving at the Ivy, John heard from Cleo that her doctor had forbidden her to step out of the hotel. Well, she must have had an amazing recovery because she was later spotted at the Back Room in the Cross in the early hours of the morning. When the incriminating shots of her, still in the Willow outfit, hit the pages of Sydney Confidential the next day, Ford immediately resigned from managing her. None of us could blame him. Cleo was now looked after by the newly formed agency Talent Inc, whose tough manager, Patrice Henry, took no rubbish from her clients.

Nevertheless, Melvin Good was really going to have his work cut out for him when he attempted to sign Cleo Jones up to The Bel Air Life. She really was super talented at being a diva. In fact, she was in a class all of her own, but since he had worked with Lindsay Lohan, he was up for anything.

Cleo and Chelsea had become such hot property that there were almost as many paps hanging around the InterContinental as there had been when Kim Kardashian was the guest of honour at a party at Hugo's shortly after she split with 'Hum Dum' – Kris Humphries, that Lurch-like husband of hers. Yes, when it came to getting a hundred percent recognition for Chelsea in Sydney, my work was done. At this rate, 'Bel Air

Babe' (the first single from her lame CD) was set to become a gay anthem. If she played her cards right, she could be the opening act of Mardi Gras, and if she camped it up just two stops more, when it came to gay icon status, she could be the next Kylie Minogue.

All the paps were trying to get the first romantic picture of the lovebirds walking arm in arm out of their suite, because there were magazines and websites in the US who were willing to pay big bucks for a shot. One of Sydney's most outrageous and aggressive paps, Roger Piper, had even booked himself into another suite on one of the executive floors so he could launch a drone over the side of the terrace with a camera and capture the action through the windows of 1560. But luck was not on his side, because each time he attempted this tricky manoeuvre the pair hadn't even been in the room.

LA-based gossip website TMZ had tracked down Chelsea's ex-boyfriend, Reggie Hunt, lead singer of nouveau-punk outfit The Rebel. Reggie had the following words of wisdom to share on video. 'Chelsea can do anything she likes, ma-an. I just want her to be happy. I don't think she ever sorta got over "the us" ending, ya know what I mean? But we both had different paths to follow.'

'Are you surprised she's taken up with another woman?' asked the TMZ reporter.

'No, ma-aan,' said Hunt. 'Love is just love. You don't pick it, it picks you.' Yeah right. Reggie's problem was that he had smoked so much Californian Gold, he was a walking fire hazard.

Not only was Chelsea's CD going nuts on iTunes but everyone was tuning into *The Bel Air Life* on Foxtel. All up, another win for Queen Bee. People hadn't stopped talking about it for days. My phone had been going non-stop with TV stations trying to secure Chelsea for an interview on everything from *Breakfast of Champions* to the daily news. She was the most fascinating personality in the city for at least a day and a half.

Of course I passed on all Chelsea's interview requests to poor Eric, who had expected to be back at his favourite table in the Chateau Marmont by now, having a double vodka cocktail. Now he would need a Patrón tequila chaser as well. If only Chelsea would just answer her fucking phone. He'd also texted her a zillion times and tried to reach her over all of her social networking sites. He'd even tried to access her room via one of the room-service waiters, but when the doorbell rang and she'd heard that familiar American accent yelling out 'Room Service!' a tad too enthusiastically, she'd refused to let him in. Poor old Eric. There was just no end to his ingenuity; if only he'd had half as good acting skills as some of his clients.

'Don't worry,' I consoled him. 'By the time they do emerge, they could probably have their own Ellen DeGeneres-style talk show.'

Eric's face immediately lit up when he heard this. 'Just how much money,' he asked, looking ridiculously hopeful, 'do you think the networks would be willing to pay?'

LOL, I had created a monster – but at least Eric was no longer threatening to sue Queen Bee. That launch party at the

Atlas was the best thing that ever happened to Chelsea – or at least it would be until Cleo showed her true colours and became the pain in the arse who we all knew and loved.

But, for now, not since Paris Hilton came to Bondi to help find a Bondi Blonde beauty queen had such a fuss been made about a reality star with such a serious deficit of talent (at least Kim Kardashian had a decent set of tits and a bum). Chelsea's girl-on-girl action was a true stroke of marketing genius.

In fact, I would have been on Sweet Street if it hadn't been for a few more nagging problems clogging up my inbox.

Despite the fact that he was an undesirable alien (or however the Department of Immigration classified those who, for a number of reasons – and when it came to Ivan there were no shortage of these – were about as popular as Justin Bieber's pet monkey flying in first class and trying to evade quarantine), Ivan Shavalik was still threatening to sue me for breach of contract – even though there was no contract signed. According to Marshall, he probably just wanted us to sling him a hundred k or for his trouble, but that was so not going to happen. This was problem number one, but as long as I didn't have any close encounters of the Russian mafia kind, I was fairly confident I could get through this with a little legal muscle.

Problem numero two was that Tod Spelsen needed to delay the launch of his beauty collection because there were apparently issues with the way the brilliantly designed packaging was being manufactured. Other people might have persevered, but 'Spello', as we now called him in the office, was particularly antsy about his 'design signature' being misread, so he'd thrown the lot out and started again. This meant we were going to get a little breathing space before the beauty launch to end all launches, but unfortunately the revised date was the day after my wedding to Michael. I would be on our honeymoon instead of spruiking Spello's lotions and potions to tout Sydney. Changing our plans was out of the question, because the invitations had already gone out and the honeymoon to the south of France was booked. If I had suggested to Michael leaving on our honeymoon a day later so I could do the launch, I knew he would have refused to marry me. He had made it very clear that our relationship and our family had to come before my work – and (especially with Fifi now in the equation) this also made perfect sense to me.

'Look, I'm really sorry,' I said when I finally got Tod on the phone at the very start of the working day in LA before Jenna had taken up her sentry position, 'October sixth is the day I'm getting married, so we definitely can't accommodate your launch on October seventh.'

'You're kidding, right?' He sounded shocked. 'Can't you cancel?'

I did the old staying-silent trick – the one I employ when I need to communicate that a suggestion is completely beyond the pale.

'Are you still there?' he asked, agitated. 'Jasmine?'

'Yes,' I responded curtly. 'I'm sorry, Tod, that's not an option. If you're totally locked into this new, revised date, then you may have to use another public relations company. Of course, I would be happy to recommend one to you.'

It was always better to get them on the back foot and pre-empt anything that might be thrown in about trying someone else.

Tod recovered well. 'Okay, I'll get back to you and let you know how we wish to proceed,' he said. 'You'll hear from us by the end of the week. Goodbye.'

And with that he was off the line. The only brownie points I had missed out on was being the first to hang up. Of course everyone knew I didn't want to lose such a potentially prestigious account, but Chelsea's launch had already put us on the map in the US. The only thing we would be missing out on with Spello was a big fat cheque for our efforts – and no doubt a major headache. But I was definitely past getting in a schvitz about it.

Problemo number three was that the lawyers and their investigators were getting close to discovering who had left the toxic messages about me all over town. Soon they were expected to press charges on my behalf, which meant I had to be prepared to go to court and testify against them. How much fun would that be, and how much would everyone be lapping it up? And what the hell was I going to wear to court? It meant precious time away from the business, and I also had to ensure the whole affair didn't come to a head during my honeymoon. The good thing was that the legal system moved as slowly as Miranda Kerr when she had sniffed out a fresh photo opportunity.

Oh, I almost forgot: the other situation clogging up
Queen Bee's inbox on a daily basis was the missives from
the ultra-stuffy Atlas Board of Owners, who kept threatening
to prosecute Queen Bee for conducting an unauthorised event
on the rooftop. That was just de-bloody-luxe. And it wasn't
as if we could call on Juliet to back us up, as she had gone
to ground faster than Richard Wilkins surprised by a gossip
columnist out on a date with a new girlfriend. (If he ran into
his nemesis Pamela Stone, you wouldn't see him for days.)

'How do we counter that?' asked Lulu when we opened
up the Atlas's ninth official letter of complaint – or was it the
tenth? Clearly the secretary of the owners' board had devoted
every waking hour since Chelsea's launch trying to get even.

'Easy,' I said, moving the correspondence into Queen Bee's
matters-pending file (aka the Too Hard Basket). 'We'll just
get the lawyers to inform the board that they're looking at a
charge of reckless endangerment for turning off the electrical
switches in the foyer. The board will also have to wear some
of the blame for allowing such a vital operations room to be
unsecured. That'll be such a shocker for them they'll almost
be begging us to have another launch there.'

Lulu looked doubtful, and maybe she had good reason to
be. My life was on steroids at the moment and I was in danger
of totally losing my grip on reality. Events were speeding up
faster than my mate Shelley on a new batch of herbal diet
pills. But somewhere in the back of my mind I believed it
would all work out okay. Maybe I was delusional from lack
of sleep, which was compounded by Fifi's latest unreasonable

compulsion for being fed at three am, and sometimes four thirty am as well.

Meanwhile, everyone in the exclusive eastern suburbs of Sydney was still preoccupied with what was going on between Chelsea and Cleo in that InterContinental suite. Would they emerge as lovers or would the clashing of those two egos be as dramatic as the seismic shift between two tectonic plates? Already, lurid tales were emerging of piercing screams of pleasure which could be heard all along the hallway.

'They've got to come out soon,' predicted Anya sagely. 'Lesbian sex is just a punishment because it never ends. It's absolutely exhausting. They'll wear themselves out.'

'Wha-at?' asked Lulu, who couldn't believe what she was hearing from the tiny brunette, one of the most demure of the Bees. Why, she never even had a drink at the end-of-year lunch.

Anya went bright red. 'Well, that's what I've heard anyway.'

Lulu and I exchanged slightly incredulous looks and she cocked her eyebrow in the way that always made me laugh. I called it her Inspector Clouseau look.

'You know what?' I said. 'I bet that when they do emerge, it'll only be a matter of time before Cleo proposes to her. Gay weddings are so hot right now. Besides she could work out an excellent deal with the Jewellery Concierge for matching diamonds. It's her favourite jeweller.

 Y

The next day was one of those days when everything seems to happen at once. Chelsea and Cleo finally emerged from their love nest and announced that Cleo would be joining *The Bel Air Life* as a special guest. Meanwhile, Eric requested that Queen Bee manage the media, which was a gift made in heaven with so many media outfits clamouring for them. Unfortunately, the only downside was that they were booked to fly out to LA in just two days, which meant there was little time to crank out anything much besides a morning slot on *Breakfast of Champions*, a mini interview on Channel 11 news and a fashion shoot for *Coco* magazine, wearing the hottest US Gen Y labels.

But the serious money came from a deal I did with *90 Minutes*, who would be following them all the way over to LA and filming them on the set of *The Bel Air Life*. It had only come about through a cross-TV channel promotion, and had earned Queen Bee so much in commission that my entire wedding flower bill – including an entire floral wall of phalaenopsis orchids by celeb florist Grandiflora – was well taken care of. It was such a coup that Cleo and Chelsea almost deserved a special credit on the wedding program.

16

I am happy to accept criticism because it helps me to develop as a human being and become a better person. I try to work harder each time I hear that what I have done is less than perfect. What I do not accept is a personal attack on my character.

Of course I am open to negative opinion, but criticise what I do and not who I am.

This was part of the victim impact statement I was asked to make in the case against the group of twenty-something-year-olds who had worked for me for a nanosecond and then decided to try to wreck my career. They must have cooked up their nasty messages to leave on different people's message banks over a few litres of no-brand vodka at the Sheaf. For all I knew, there was an 'I Was Dumped from Queen Bee' support group who met there every week. The lawyers had been able to trace the group through the calls. No doubt they had thought they could get away with it because the calls had been made from a prepaid sim, but of course it was traceable. The investigators not only found out where it had been purchased but when, and then a review of the security footage at the shop where the sim was purchased almost certainly revealed Holly, who had worked for me for a short time before basically everything that was not nailed down went missing. Holly wasn't smart enough to throw the sim away but used the phone to stay in touch with other members of the group, including Kelly Young. The investigators looking into the case said that the girls were almost shitting themselves about what they had done. Most of the group involved were former private school girls from good families, who were now definitely going to pay. It was just a question of how much.

The lawyers had asked me to write the victim impact statement because it would help to put the slander into some sort of context for the courts. They needed to know that this was not just another case of tit for tat but something that cut much deeper. I had spent some time thinking about it and writing down how it had affected me.

'Jazzy, you look as though you've just been told they'll be finally winding up Chanel,' Lulu wisecracked.

I hadn't noticed the small blonde entering the room where I had been working since sparrow's-fart. We had arranged to meet in the office to put the finishing touches on the new proposal for Spello's launch so we could make the working day in LA. (Spello had eventually decided that despite the date problems, we were right for the job, which may or may not have had something to do with the groundswell of publicity for Chelsea.) The launch of Spello's beauty collection was now taking place at the beginning of November, right in time for Sydney's pre-Christmas buying frenzy. We wanted the collection to be front and centre on everyone's holiday shopping list.

We would be setting up a marquee deep in the grounds of the Botanic Gardens with a theme of 'Midnight in the Garden of Love'. Of course, it would only be a cocktail party that would be done and dusted by eight thirty pm, but all the guests would believe that midnight had just struck in the fucking Hanging Gardens of Babylon because the marquee would be lit a rich, deep, dark blue. Orchid trees would have a starring role, and by the time we had finished propping there would be none left in the markets. We also wanted to source some gardenias in full bloom. Our preferred florist, Grandiflora, was going to have a field day. Once we got the budget approved by Spello's LA office, we could get Sydney's best party engineers started on it.

With the concept all sorted, I had time to work on my special statement. Yes, the victim impact statement – although a victim was the last thing I felt like right now. Harassed, yes; stressed, absolutely; but victimised? Please. At least not when I could see that the people behind this were basically pathetic. At a guess, my ex-employees' summer breaks in Europe would be cancelled quick smart once their parents started to cop the court costs and the mega damages bill for slander. The only problem was that I couldn't talk to anyone about the plans to sue or the identity of the people behind the obnoxious messages because it was going to be before the courts and so the names couldn't get out in the media. My pal Luke had been nagging me about it for weeks but I had to keep changing the subject each time he asked.

'It'll be so fine, Jazz, I promise,' he said last time he brought it up, over lunch at China Doll. 'We won't identify them, promise. Just give us the names and I swear not to publish them.'

'No can do, Luke,' I said, laughing as I speared a particularly plump prawn and put it on my plate. 'I can't do that, not even for you – but what I can say is that it's def going to be almost as juicy as my chilli prawn.'

Once Lulu and I had pressed the send button on Spello's precious proposal, we decided to review some of the loaner cars, which belonged to our car client, Panther.

Certain publications were loaned cars with the name of the magazine on the car doors – it was a genius way of publicising Panther cars and linking them to some of the best, most aspirational titles around. Plus it was a real bonus for some of our favoured clients in mag-land who got the use of a car for free and saved themselves a shitload of money each week. All they had to pay for was the petrol and any fines they incurred, which is where it all went wrong, especially when it came to Amber Jallani, fashion director for Chic magazine. From the look of the parking fines that were coming in on a daily basis, Amber didn't believe in parking stations, or meters for that matter, since she routinely parked for hours in No Stopping zones.

Amber's sporty Panther 320 was currently in for servicing and to straighten out a few of the mysterious bumps that had appeared on the chassis. These had to be sorted out immediately because having a battered car out there was not a good look for either Panther or Chic.

Unfortunately, all those parking fines Amber had accrued had landed on the client's desk, as Panther was still registered as the owner of the vehicle, and they had shot them back to Queen Bee with the order that they be paid straight away.

Now Frances, Amber's PA, was getting stroppy on her behalf to have the car returned, but what she didn't seem to grasp was that it couldn't go back until Chic or Amber coughed up for the fines.

At first the emails were civil-ish:

Amber needs her car returned pronto because she's going on a fashion shoot to Palm Beach this week and wants to drive it.

Lulu, who was Panther's account executive, told Frances that the car was ready to be collected or it could be dropped off at Chic, but first those pesky fines had to be sorted out. Frances chose to ignore this information. *Please have the car sent around to Chic's offices no later than midday today*, she ordered.

Certainly, Lulu responded. Once you pay the parking fines by cheque or credit card.

There was a cessation of communication for ninety minutes. It looked like a stalemate.

But no, Frances then came back online. *I have spoken with Amber and she said she knows nothing about the fines. Please deliver the car pronto or Amber might have to consider going with another car company. Mercedes has been desperate to get her behind the wheel of their latest model.*

Bullshit. The way Amber drove she was lucky anyone gave her a car at all. But even Lulu wasn't ready for the next development, when a flustered Carla from Panther Cars rang to advise that Frances was in reception and was apparently insisting on picking up Amber's sporty wheels.

'Tell her to pay the parking fines on the spot and please deal with Queen Bee in future,' Lulu ranted.

Unfortunately, Frances had no Chic credit card on her or the cash – in fact, she had only enough money to cover the cab back to the office. But all's well that ends well. Magically, the fines were paid the same afternoon and Lulu was happy to drop back Amber's shiny restored car herself with an extra-big smile for Frances. The accounts department for Chic was just lucky they didn't have to pay for the repairs as well, although perhaps it would have taught Amber not to treat her wheels like a dodgem car.

It would be great to be able to say that Frances had learnt not to pressure Queen Bee when it came to freebies, but sadly this was not the case. The following week she fired off an email to Lulu with another request.

Dear Lulu,

Amandine is holding a celebratory drink tonight to thank the fashion team for a fantastic shoot in Tahiti and she was wondering where she could source some French champagne. She just needs six bottles.

Thanks so much for all your help,

Frances Lilly (on behalf of Amandine Grice, editor-in-chief of *Chic*)

And there it was. *Chic* magazine was apparently so hard up that they couldn't even afford the office drinks. Queen Bee didn't even have a French champagne client, but declining had to be a diplomatic effort.

Dear Frances,

How exciting that *Chic* did so well on the Tahitian shoot. All of us at Queen Bee cannot wait to see the pages. Please congratulate everyone on our behalf.

The drinks sound wonderful but we are unclear about whether you were actually inviting Jasmine to attend in your recent email. If so, I shall have to check her diary.

Unfortunately we do not currently have a French champagne client but we would be very happy to send round a crate of sparkling L'Eau mineral water and some packages of Canape Curls – the latest product from Byron

Bay Cookies, which will be launching next month. You
will be the first to try them.

Kind regards,

Lulu (on behalf of Jasmine Lewis)

For some reason we didn't hear back from Frances, which
was rude considering our generous offers. But then this was
probably because Frances took it upon herself to try to organise
some champagne as she couldn't be bothered trying to get
the money from petty cash and stepping out of the office
to buy it herself. Amandine would have been mortified if
she knew exactly what her PA was up to — but one of these
days we would find a way of letting her know all about the
state of play.

We were always happy to keep plugging L'Eau, but it
had been particularly rugged lately trying to align the brand
with the style elite. In fact, we almost exchanged blows with
Sam Fenzno, the overblown, drug-fucked publicist who was
working on the launch of Le Jean (St Tropez's leading jeans
brand, soon to hit the shelves of Myer). The launch was taking
place at Otto, and L'Eau had provided the water for every table;
the brief from the client was to get the distinctive water in the
hands of as many celebrities as possible.

Or at least it was until Fenzno suddenly inserted himself
in front of our friendly pap Marco's lens and threw up his
hands dramatically. 'Sorry, mate, this is a private event,' he
said in that whiny voice of his. 'Tell Jasmine that she'll have
to try and plug her water brand somewhere else.'

It took all of thirty seconds for Marco to relay this message back to me on his mobile, and a hundred and twenty more for me to be in front of Sam, hands on my hips.

'What's going on, Sam?' I demanded, sounding as aggressive as I felt as the cream of the social set moved past us to their tables.

'Now, Jazzy,' he said, trying to placate me, 'you know this is our event and not yours. It's not really the time and the place for any more cross-promotion.'

I looked at the big, bloated man in front of me who clearly thought he was all that and then some. I stared at his hairy gut bursting from the bottom half of his sweat-soaked Ralph Lauren shirt as he shuffled uncomfortably on his feet.

Fortunately, Jeff, Otto's maître d', happened to be passing by at that very moment.

'Hi, Jeff.' I smiled winningly (Michael and I were regular clients at Otto – it was where we liked to eat most of our meals).

'Miss Jasmine!' he responded warmly. He always addressed me like that – it was our private joke.

'Hi, Jeff,' Sam butted in, 'everything is just perfect for our event tonight. Thanks so much.'

'Good.' Jeff was faintly friendly but professional. 'Let me know if you need anything.'

'Actually we do, Jeff,' I said with another killer smile. 'Would you mind removing all the bottles of L'Eau from the tables? I'm afraid there's been a mistake.'

'No, no, no, don't do that!' said Sam, raising his voice to such a level that guests still filing to their tables stopped in their tracks.

Apparently Sam's budget for the Le Jean launch didn't stretch to six hundred for mineral water. The colour had drained from his florid face. 'Please, Jazzy,' he pleaded. 'No need to be rash.'

'Okay, but only if you point out to Marco the celebs who would be happy to pose with a bottle of L'Eau in their hand.'

Sam looked as though he might explode but then he nodded. 'Of course.'

'So I shall leave the bottles where they are then?' asked Jeff, who had been waiting patiently during this exchange.

I nodded back sweetly at him and gave him a wink.

Only one person declined to be in our shots, the international stylist Ginger B, who declared that she didn't 'do consumer'. We could live without her seal of approval anyway. But, really, us Bees have gotta do what we gotta do, and if we need those bottles of mineral water in people's hands, then don't get in our way. Our lives and red-soled shoes depend on it.

17

As if there wasn't already enough to worry about, in the lead-up to the wedding some deviant attempted to get my credit card details through the florist who was taking care of the arrangements for my big day. Jeez, wasn't anything sacred anymore? When was the universe going to cut me some slack? If I'd cared to consult my Jewish grandmother about all this she would definitely say that I was cursed. But unfortunately Bubbe was already down on me for having Fifi before the marriage ('Oy vey, what a schmuck you are! This would never have happened if you had dated a nice Jewish boy'). She would have then reverted to her customary habit of talking in the third person in order to further lament my situation and, more importantly, hers – as in: 'Bubbe doesn't know how she will be able to face her friends in the Bridge

Club again with a granddaughter who is a nebish. Nu, she can't do something as simple as getting married before she has the baby.'

Ah yes, if I picked up the hotline to Bubbe central it would be on for young and old, so best just deal with it myself.

Flowers had definitely become a thing with our wedding. Think Midnight in the Garden of Love and then some. Thanks to Churchill Brooks, our excitable wedding planner, Michael and I would be taking our vows in front of a floral backdrop composed of a wall of orchids, jasmine (of course), wild roses and tuberoses. The Oscars red carpet never had it so good. There was also to be a small field of roses on each side of the driveway leading up to Quay restaurant, petals strewn over the pathway, and inside there would be a vase on every table. The flower bill alone was costing more than some entire wedding budgets. What the hell, I was hopefully marrying Michael for life; this was no time for half-measures.

But back to the florist and the mysterious email which had been sent to me from the florist's office requesting the security question on my credit card.

The florist rang me. 'I've had my security guy look into this and it seems that an external party has intercepted the details within the email correspondence, and attempted to make their email look like a Visa verification request – although these are never done via email. When he sends through his findings, I'll forward them on to you.'

Great, it wasn't just the haters out there who were trying to destroy my business but someone was trying to rob me as well. Just how many black cats had crossed my path? It wasn't so much that they had been successful in siphoning funds from my credit card, it's that they had attempted to, but better luck next time because that credit card had just been cancelled. It was a pain in the arse but it had to be done.

'Bud, don't worry about it,' Shelley said over the phone when I called her to wallow about being marooned up shit creek without a Louis Vuitton paddle. 'That kind of fucked-up shit happens to me all the time. Just ignore it and carry on. Now we need to talk about your hen's party. It's happening.'

I stared at the sheaf of papers on my desk. There were so many matters pending that I'd soon have to find an entire new filing cabinet to contain them.

'Shelley,' I said, exasperated, 'I only just have enough time to squeeze in the wedding and the honeymoon, let alone those kind of extracurricular activities.'

'Don't worry about a thing,' she said agreeably. 'Leave it all to me. I'm thinking the luxury spa at The Darling, dinner at Black by Ezard and then Marquee. Plus a few other tricks that I have up my sleeve.'

There was nothing Shelley liked better than to party and spend to excess. Somewhere out there a small South American country had been robbed of its entire budget to support Shelley's black Amex.

But I had my own budget problems trying to rein in Churchill Brooks, who had heard all about the Vera Wang shopping expedition in LA from Shelley's Twitter and Instagram feeds and had clearly decided that this was the wedding to try out all the stunts which he had been held back on in the past because of budget restraints. Churchill was brilliant at racking up bills; he could always find new ways of spending money – like employing a troupe of jugglers and dancers to keep the guests amused between the ceremony and the reception while the bridal party were being snapped and filmed by a budding Australian film director and cinematographer he had found among the graduating class at NIDA two years ago.

Another of his schemes was to have the bridal party arrive at Quay on a super yacht decked out in yellow and white bunting, accompanied by fireboats with ceremonial sprays of water spurting out as if from a whale's gills. Sadly for Churchill, this was not an option.

'We're staying next door at the Park Hyatt,' I reminded him. 'So we're just going to jump in some hire cars for a five-minute drive around the corner. That's as flashy as it will get.'

Who did he think Michael and I were – a couple of Greek shipping tycoons? There was also Fifi to consider. She was going to be part of the wedding party and I didn't think she would like to look back on attending her very first wedding, for her parents, arriving by boat like a member of the royal family. It could traumatise her for life if there were so many things going on in one day.

'Hmm,' Churchill said, looking pensive, which of course was just him thinking about another way of adding an extra twenty k to the bill. 'How about choppering in? That could be very chic. I don't think anyone has done that before.'

'With good reason,' I responded, casually flicking through his portfolio of past clients' events and scrutinising their faces to see if I recognised anyone. (Luke would love some detail on those untouchable events in the Sydney social scene.) Was that a sitting room in James Packer's new Vaucluse mansion? It was hard to tell without looking too interested and alerting Churchill to what I was up to. But, LOL, I couldn't imagine Packer allowing one of his events to be included in a wedding planner's album; he was far too private for that. Come to think of it, I couldn't imagine him dealing with Churchill at all. Somehow I imagined that any event guru to the Packer family would have to be much calmer and less given to perspiration issues. Churchill sweated up a storm, even when most people were shivering in the air conditioning. His internal body-cooling system had short-circuited and was officially as overblown as his bills.

Churchill decided to concentrate instead on the calligraphy for the hundred and twenty guests' menus and place cards. He also wanted to give everyone a special handmade candle from Paris, worth a hundred bucks each.

'Keith Urban will be in town at that time getting ready for a concert at the Opera House three nights later. I think we should try to book him in for the wedding – even if he does just two songs . . .' he started.

'Um, earth to Churchill: Keith Urban gave up doing weddings twenty-five years ago. You might as well try and get One Direction to pop in.' I couldn't quite believe it when

223

I saw him quickly note something down on his pad. What was he going to come up with next – Bono?

It would have been good to have the luxury of taking time off to organise the wedding just like your typical bridezilla, but it wasn't to be. Everyone's favourite female gay couple, Chelsea and Cleo, made sure of that by phoning to say they were on their way back to Sydney.

'Filming has wrapped up on *The Bel Air Life* for season three,' Chelsea explained, 'and the sales of the CD have been so strong in Australia that we figured we should come back here and do a bit more promotion. Plus, I want to see more of Cleo's home base.'

'And you're ringing me because . . . ?' I said, growing impatient with yet another excerpt from Lifestyles of the Lovesick and Famous.

'We want you to handle the media because Eric can't get away this time,' Chelsea said brightly, not registering that I might be a little over the juicy twosome. 'And, what's more, we've heard that you're having a wedding and we'd like to perform for you. It's the least we can do, after all you've done for us.'

Wha-at? I was flabbergasted. There was silence on the line for a little more time than was polite.

'No, no, that's sooo sweet of you,' I spluttered eventually. 'Too sweet actually.'

My internal calculator was going into meltdown as I tried to figure out how much this generous gesture would cost me. No doubt it would mean extra security, a green room and the rider from hell. Cleo was fond of insisting on vintage Billecart-Salmon, no less than a crate – not that she ever got through it all. At least, not during an official gig anyway. And I could just imagine how it would all go down with Michael's mum, Fiona, and all her establishment friends who would be rocking up to the wedding. They were only now just getting used to the fact that it looked like I was here to stay. I didn't need the hottest global lesbian double act around to seal the deal that I was def a bad influence on my soon-to-be husband.

'We're not charging you a cent,' Chelsea continued cheer-fully, as if she was offering me the bargain of the year. 'All we would need is two return airfares. Cleo wants to go first class but I'm happy to go business. Anyway, she said you have zillions of frequent flyer points so it won't be coming out of your pocket anyway.'

'What!!' I couldn't help emitting a slight scream of alarm, which was probably nothing compared to the sound that would escape from Michael's mouth when he heard the news about the wedding entertainment and the frequent flyer deficit that would go along with it.

I started coughing theatrically. 'Sorry, Chelsea, allergies.' Cough, splutter. 'I'll call you back in half an hour, once I get rid of this tickle in my throat.'

18

You only get married once in your life. At least, that was the plan for me, because with Michael I had everything, including our beautiful baby daughter, Fifi. And, well, who else would put up with such a fabulously frenetic life as mine? You almost had to be a human Mogadon.

Speaking of the nuptials, Queen Bee's phones were ringing red hot with peeps who thought they should have been invited to my wedding but weren't. Talk about freaks. What was wrong with these desperadoes? This was a wedding ceremony involving family and close friends, not a scent launch. And yet each morning in the lead-up to the big day, Queen Bee's message bank was filled with the hushed tones of people who thought they should have been invited despite the fact that I hardly knew them – or, in the case of Wally Grimes, wish that I didn't.

'Snazzy Jazzy,' he bleated down the line in the early hours of the morning, the only time he could be sure that no one would be in the office so he wouldn't have to put his outrageous request live to one of the Bees. 'My invitation to your wedding appears to have been lost in the mail, sweetie. But, don't worry, because I shall be able to make it. See you in church, Jazzy; and you don't mind, do you, if I bring Jasper along? He's dying to see you in that very expensive Vera Wang. Any chance that you could pop it on for a picture beforehand? We'll only publish it as you walk down the aisle.'

It takes a lot to get me gobsmacked – I've got the sort of gob that smacks first and asks questions later. But this had all but floored me. Wally Grimes had recently taken great delight in the toxic message campaign. He'd run it as a lead with the most unflattering pictures of me he could find and a headline that read 'Poisonous Publicist to the Stars Felled by Toxic Messages'. There was absolutely no way he was coming to the wedding, and I would let him know this the same way that he had put the request to me – by leaving something on his message bank in the early hours of the morning, when he would no doubt be out gorging on the good life somewhere. Wally was so bloated from freeloading at lavish events that none of his jackets buttoned up properly.

'Hi, Wally, good to hear from you,' I said sweetly into his answer phone early the next morning. 'Thank you for your enquiry about my wedding, but unfortunately your invitation didn't get lost in the mail. I never sent one in the first place because we're limited in numbers to just family and friends. Also, while I would love to do some pictures for you – and thank you for asking – there just isn't time because I'm working right up until the date. I'm very flattered that you're interested though. Let me know if there's anything else I can do. Bye bye.'

Others who were begging for an invite included Narelle Brooks, a junior fashion editor at *Zest*, whom I had worked with closely on a shoot with Allison Palmer. We had got along well but clearly not as well as she thought when she rang to see whether she could score a wedding invite. Narelle was salivating because she had heard that there would be a fabulous goodie bag. Lulu let her down gently by telling her that she was waitlisted and sending her out a pair of the new-season Mavi jeans.

Ye gods, if you could call a hundred-dollar candle a goodie bag, then a goodie bag it was, but wedding guests who were hoping for one of the signature Queen Bee bags – containing ModelCo tanning products, Benefit brow packs, L'Eau mineral water and a Trelise Cooper scarf – were going to be seriously disappointed, Then again, our goodie bags were so heavy, you needed a trolley to take them to your ride. These were not usually available at Quay.

We were just putting together the final preparations when we received the most disturbing proposition of all. Diane Wilderstein let it be known that she wanted to come to the wedding since she was the person who had given me my start in PR. Yeah right, I almost needed therapy after a spell in her office. The only thing she did for me was to make me determined not to work for a nutcase again; in fact, not to work for anyone else at all.

Even more outrageous, Wilderstein tried to leverage her way in by way of her great pal Lillian Richard, editor of *Eve Pascal*, who was one of the most important people in the fashion industry – but that was five years ago now. Lillian was invited to the wedding (anything to get on her good side, especially as we still wanted an *Eve Pascal* cover for Allison) and she let Lulu know that she would like to bring Diane Wilderstein as her plus one. Lulu had to tell her as delicately as possible there were no plus ones to this wedding.

The whole situation was getting out of hand, so I asked Pamela Stone to write something in her column about the number of high-profile identities desperate to come to my wedding, hinting broadly as to their names. I thought that would end it there, but I soon found out it was only the beginning as I was to find out on the very day of the wedding.

'We should have got married on a remote island and then had a big party when we returned from the honeymoon,' said Michael. 'That would have been the civilised way to do it. These people are absolute fruitcakes.'

Me too, especially because I had let Shelley talk me into that hen's party – an outdated concept if ever there was one – I don't care how chic Jodi Gordon's and Jennifer Hawkins' were when they married their respective partners. Like those two glamazons, my party was taking place within the relatively safe confines of The Darling, the luxe hotel at The Star. Damn Shelley for being so persuasive.

'I've booked us a bloody big suite at The Darling and it'll just be very chilled,' she promised. 'Nothing tacky, we're not even going to the restaurants at Star, but I've organised for a chef from Momofuku to prepare dinner for us in the kitchen.'

'What kitchen?' I asked, unable to keep up.

'Oh, it comes with the suite – it's more of a penthousey thing actually,' she said. 'And don't worry, I have it all covered. It's my gift to you as your fave bridesmaid – even if you wouldn't let me wear that Chanel gown I wanted.'

Just as well; it didn't come in her size, but I certainly wasn't going to be the one to remind Shelley that she was only a size zero in her head – definitely not in her hips.

In the end, the hen's party was anything but chilled and ended up with three of the Bees, led by Lulu, forcibly removed from The Star by security.

This is how it went down. A few of the Bees decided that it would be fun to have a little excursion from The Darling to The Star's gambling floor because they had never had so much as a flutter before. (Some of my critics would say that it was a big enough risk for them to be working for me in the first place.) They were just making their way to the roulette wheel when they spotted a well-known married TV chef and a young female soapie star making out in a dark corner near a row of poker machines. The pair must have escaped from the first-night audience of *Legally Blonde*, which was opening next door at The Star's theatre. Quick as a flash (no pun intended),

Lulu snapped the couple on her Instagram with the aim of sending it straight to Luke Jefferson.

The Bees weren't to know that there's a no-photo policy at The Star, but no sooner had they got the shot than they were apprehended by security, who strong-armed them out of the casino and made them delete the photo. This was grossly unfair. Queen Bee employees have been taught never to adhere to the rules, because as everyone knows, the ones who follow the rules finish last. This was why Anya, who was behind Lulu, had swiftly fired off another shot when security was busy with Lulu and just before the couple finally woke up to what was going on (they had been so lip-locked they almost had to be surgically separated). Thanks to Anya, Luke absolutely owned the front page of *The Sun* the next day, and while Michael and his mates came away from his stag night with monumental hangovers, we had used my hen's party for good. (I'm not entirely sure the loved-up couple would agree with that, but at least the soapie star lost her goodie two-shoes image and started to be offered much grittier roles.)

And thanks to Shelley's indulgent pre-hen's party shopping spree, I would be wearing the latest collection of La Perla lingerie beneath my wedding gown.

19

People get married every day at The Rocks beneath the shadow of the Harbour Bridge and right across from the Sydney Opera House – it's a cheesy backdrop but it does the trick with the folks back home in downtown Tokyo or Shanghai. For me it was all about luxury – Michael and I were huge fans of the restaurant Quay, where it takes almost as long to get a table on a Saturday night as it does to get a Birkin bag outta Hermès. It's like a temple of haute cuisine – so why not stage a semi-religious event there? It was my personal take on an *Eat, Pray, Love* moment, only back to front.

Sadly, I couldn't book out Quay for an entire Saturday night – not unless Michael and I decided to postpone our nuptials until the year 2020. So we were getting hitched on a Sunday afternoon, with a lunch at Quay for our guests and the ceremony on the top floor, where 'Churchy' had outdone himself creating the wall of very expensive flowers. Altars are sooo last year, after all, and there's something not quite right about using one when you have a wedding celebrant doing the honours.

I'd like to report that the scene inside the Park Hyatt where the bridal party was getting ready for the big moment was as zen as the lead-up to a typical Akira Isogawa show, which is all about poetry in motion and less is more. But it wasn't. It was chaos.

Shelley started the day by cracking open a few bottles of rare Dom Pérignon rose for us to sip with breakfast.

'Come on, Jazz,' she cooed, 'this will make everything so much more mellow, and we have to celebrate the fact that you're leaving singledom once and for all.'

'Um, hello, didn't we do that at the hen's party?' I replied. 'You remember, the night when Lulu and Anya were almost carried out of The Star. I think their photos have now been circulated to the casino's security team with a big stripe across their faces showing they're banned for life.'

'That's okay, some of the restaurants there are overrated,' said Shelley, who had made a study of Sydney's best eateries. She could give a paper on it at the next Gastronomic Convention and have the audience eating out of her hand.

In the end, besides Shell, the people who consumed most of the Dom were the hair and makeup team. Clovis and Annita were the best in the business, and they had a corner of the suite set aside just like the backstage area at Fashion Week. Lulu, who was also a bridesmaid, barely touched a glass because she knew that she needed to stay alert for even the most benign events involving Queen Bee; and Jackie, another school friend of Shell's and mine who was in the bridal party as a matron of honour, didn't drink because she was pregnant.

'You really ought to let me do an updo for a change,' Clovis said for the eighth time that morning. 'You'll look like more of a princess in that Vera Wang gown.' He held out a row of blonde extensions that would certainly give me the bun from hell.

'Nah, I want to look like me but with one of your signature blowdries.'

He eventually gave up on the idea but it was tough going for a while.

The good news was that although Chelsea and Cleo had held out for a few days for plane tickets to attend the wedding (which they had not been invited to – a small detail), when I was unable to accommodate their request they had found someone else to sponsor their trip anyway. They were both going to be the brand ambassadors for the OceanBlue XXX collection of swimwear for the bold and daring.

But for some reason they were still determined to attend the wedding.

'We would never have met if it wasn't for you,' Chelsea declared over the phone from LA. Which was kinda true; but, then again, if they hadn't got on so well in that lift they would both be suing me for a raft of charges, including reckless endangerment for letting them get stuck in there in the first place.

The upshot was that they were coming to the wedding whether we liked it or not but they would not be performing, so there would be no green room required and no massive rider.

Instead, David Anvill, my good buddy and co-host of *Breakfast of Champions* – as well as being a recording artist – was going to sing a couple of romantic songs. He was refusing payment. 'It'll be my wedding gift to you,' he insisted. 'It'll be a privilege just to be there.'

So good all round. Unfortunately, what I hadn't bargained for was that Chelsea and Cleo had checked into the Park Hyatt as well, so there was a paparazzi storm outside straining to get a shot of the loved-up couple walking through the foyer on their way to the wedding.

As the cherub of honour, Fifi was having her own moment: she didn't want to wear her custom Allison Palmer frock for the ceremony. We had two outfits and both seemed to leave her underwhelmed, judging by the kicking and screaming that was going on as Anna was trying to dress her.

The problem with the hair and makeup team drinking champagne so early in the day was that they needed so many chasers afterwards in the form of strong cups of coffee. The bad news about coffee is that it can stain badly when spilt.

And so it was that seconds after I had finally got into my Vera Wang wedding gown, Nenne, one of the junior assistants, took a quick swig of her coffee then dropped the cup, which made a huge arc in the air, sending coffee flying.

'Oh my fucking God!' she shrieked, 'I am so, so sorry!'

'Nenne! Nenne! What have you done?' Clovis shrieked even louder, at which Nenne burst into tears.

'I didn't mean to, it just slipped,' she wailed.

For a moment the room went horribly still as I inspected my gown for coffee splatters. Everything seemed to go in slow motion as Shelley and my mum, who had both rushed over, scrutinised every ruffle – but thankfully it was spotless. The coffee had missed me by millimetres.

'That's okay, Nenne,' I tried to reassure the young girl, who was now a quivering, sobbing wreck. 'But for now, I want everyone to step away from their cups of coffee and any kind of food and drink at all besides Evian. Is that clear?'

'Yes, Jasmine,' they all replied in unison.

Was that near miss with the coffee a symbol for what was to unfold later that day? Either way, almost from that moment on, things became as deeply interesting as a ride on the Slide From Hell – the latest attraction at Wet'n'Wild.

When my bridesmaids and I finally made our way downstairs at the Park Hyatt and into the Rolls-Royce, there seemed to be paps everywhere, which was crazy because Chelsea and Cleo had already left for Quay and were waiting there with the other guests. But it seemed that since the great toxic message scandal I was a celebrity.

'What the hell is your problem?' said Shelley to the scrum of snappers, almost elbowing one in the face as she got into the car. She was outraged on my behalf because Fifi, who had been coaxed into her Adrienne & The Misses Bonney dress, was crying from all the fuss.

'We're just doing our job, luv,' said one beret-wearing bloke I didn't recognise. Yeah right.

It takes approximately one and a half minutes to drive from the Park Hyatt to Quay, but we had to spend around half an hour circling the block because we couldn't even get close to the restaurant, there were so many paps outside snapping Chelsea and Cleo, who were loving every minute of it.

Churchill was standing outside the restaurant, watching helplessly. 'This is an outrage,' he squealed into his walkie-talkie. In the car with me, Lulu was holding the second two-way – she sure was a very hands-on bridesmaid. 'If we don't get things underway soon, the flowers will start melting in the heat. It's about forty degrees here.'

Indeed, Churchy was already one hot perspiring mess and no amount of clean Hermès hankies were going to mop him down.

'I'm going to call the police, they're just around the corner. Maybe they'll give you a police escort to your own wedding,' he said hopefully.

Now that was something I hadn't planned for but would love. A police escort! How wonderfully OTT would that be? Perfect for News at Nine. 'See what you can do,' I relayed to him. I could see him jumping up and down as we circled the block for the fourth time.

But it turned out that the police had other things on their to-do list that day. And, anyway, the problem was partially solved when the couple finally stopped pouting and preening and made their way inside with the rest of the guests.

At last the Rolls was able to nose its way in and let me out right in front of the red carpet, which led all the way to the upstairs terrace. At a signal from Churchill, a string quartet began the first notes of the bridal march. I looked at the room, which was lush enough to belong to a chateau perched in the south of France, and at the faces of the people I loved – it was perfect. And there was Michael looking impossibly handsome and proud as he waited for me in front of the wall of flowers (there mustn't have been a single stem left at Grandiflora that day). Even Fifi seemed to understand how special the occasion was and looked as serene as a Miss Bonney-clad angel in Shell's arms. Weddings, I thought to myself as a flutter of nerves suddenly took hold of me, were underrated – this was just heaven.

It was when the entire wedding party was assembled in front of the guests and we were halfway through our vows that it happened. Suddenly a man in a leather jacket and wearing mirrored shades walked into the upstairs room at Quay. At first I thought he was a rubbernecking tourist – although I noticed that he did look a bit nervous.

'Are you Miss Jasmine Lewis?' he asked, awkwardly walking down the aisle, squishing Churchill's carefully created trail of rose petals with his heavy boots. Funny the things that go through your head at critical moments; instead of worrying about what the man was up to, I was just wondering how much the ruined carpet would add to the bill. What with

Ella Von Scandale's white silk carpet and now potentially this one – it had been a very bad year for ruined rugs at Queen Bee.

It was only when Fifi started to cry again and Michael inserted himself in the man's path that I began worrying we could all be in danger.

'This is a private event, mate,' said my dad, quickly stepping in as well, as the room suddenly started to buzz with noise.

The man ignored both Michael and my dad and handed me a piece of paper tied with a pink ribbon. 'You've now been served in a suit brought against you by Mr Ivan Shavalik,' he announced. 'I suggest you contact your solicitor.'

That tireless attention-seeker Cleo was first on her feet. 'This is an outrage,' she bellowed, while beside her, Chelsea, surprisingly demure in a silk Etro dress, remained seated but nodded vigorously.

'Someone throw out this intruder, or I'll do it myself,' Cleo continued, turning around to give everyone a three-hundred-and-sixty-degree view of her this-season's electric blue 'D&G' corset dress, which the Italian duo had created with the idea of highlighting body art (okay, tramp stamps) just like Cleo's to perfection.

The process server barely blinked at the outburst but marched back down the aisle, leaving greasy footprints among the squished rose petals. He disappeared as fast as he had arrived.

Churchill, who had been hovering in the wings, looked as though he was about to have a heart attack. The precious 'aisle' which he had created had been destroyed. But what to do? Should he instruct his crew to surreptitiously roll it up while the guests' attention was diverted elsewhere or should he just leave it where it was but scatter another layer of perfumed petals over the footprints? And just where were the spare rose petals anyway? They were supposed to be blown up into the air the moment Michael and I had signed the registry and were making our way to a secluded space on the upper deck for more photographs. (Light-reflecting screens had been set up to shield the bridal party from tourists but to allow for the backdrop of the Sydney Opera House. The hair and makeup team were currently setting up their stations with power packs to allow them to use all their equipment.)

Yes, Churchill was in the mother of all flaps because of the vile intrusion on the wedding, which he had already earmarked for a very special spot in his portfolio. It had to be picture perfect. Finally he made the decision to leave the carpet where it was and scatter the rest of the rose petals, while his assistant hurried off to find some more.

'You have ten minutes max,' he yelled, thrusting a hundred-dollar note in her hand. 'And don't get that awful deep red variety, because they will only look common,' he cautioned.

The wedding celebrant, a man in his sixties with slicked-back longish silvery-blond hair, delicately cleared his throat to bring everyone back to the matter at hand, his face as pink as if it had been recently plunged into hot water. He was wearing a sombre dark suit but, in honour of the occasion, a light pink damask shirt with a red string bow tie. In other circumstances he might have held the attention of some of the guests, who would have idly speculated about his sexuality. But for now there was just too much going on.

'This is most unusual,' he remarked, sounding kind and looking concerned. It wasn't quite as bad as the bride or groom being left at the altar, but it was definitely up there as a major dampener on the festivities. 'Michael, Jasmine, are you ready to proceed?' he asked. 'If you are, I suggest you put any thoughts about what has just happened right out of your mind. They have no place here, because this is your day,' he added, trying to sound upbeat.

Michael and I looked at each other, still a little stunned, and I winked ostentatiously, as much for our guests' sake as for Michael's. I was all about putting on a brave face.

'Yes,' we both said at the same time. This broke the ice.

'Proceed,' I shouted gleefully, to reassure everyone that this was not getting me down but inside I was in absolute turmoil. First, my impending birth threatened to upstage Fashion Week, and now my wedding was turning into a circus. Couldn't I do anything right? I also thought that Michael may want to kill me when this was all over. He was all for taking the Jennifer Hawkins' option and getting married on a beach in Bali with only our nearest and dearest.

All this kerfuffle was too much for one elderly woman in the back row, one of Michael's relatives, who seemed to buckle over in her seat. But she was quickly revived before she actually fainted. Just as well, or she would have missed out on the next dramatic development. The service soon got underway again, to the cheers of the crowd – egged on by

Shelley – but almost immediately, a surprised hush fell over the congregation. Images started to move on the white walls next to the celebrant, as though a film projector had been switched on. At first it was hard to make out what it was, and I stared at it blankly. But then the images became clear. Someone had surreptitiously filmed my undignified exit from Fashion Week when my waters broke.

After a few moments of murmured consternation, everyone turned around to see who was playing the video only to see a shadowy figure in a hoodie run off – his job done. Then this: 'Fuckkkk!' The bloodcurdling scream that escaped Diane's Wilderstein's lips as her ankle twisted was a dead giveaway.

Bugger those YSL Tributes, because they tripped up the culprit just as she was legging it towards the escalators, making her escape to the busy precinct below where a car was idling in wait. We found out later that the driver had been instructed to keep the motor running and under no circumstances to move away from the agreed pick-up point.

By the time a panting and puffing Churchill and the security detail caught up with her, Diane presented an even less dignified appearance than I had when my waters broke. With the blonde wig covering her trademark ratty black bob completely skewed and a split in her 'vintage' Chanel suit (since the decline in her business, she could hardly afford to keep up with the new collection), she looked downright tragic. Somehow, she had managed to camouflage herself among the guests and had got close enough to the action to play the video. Far too vain to wear flats with her best ensemble, in her deluded state she had somehow convinced herself that she was still young and sprightly enough to run in heels. But those days were over.

Diane Wilderstein's misadventure left Churchill and the security team in a quandary. Who to call first – an ambulance (she definitely couldn't get up), or the police? She could surely be charged with public nuisance and trespassing on a private event. There were also privacy issues to do with her relaying the Fashion Week footage. (But we would probably struggle to get this one up – after all, this was the sort of thing the Bees got up to most days in the interests of making money and keeping all of our journalism contacts happy.)

These close relationships definitely paid off, because in the newspapers' online editions that afternoon and in the following day's paper, the reports of the wedding were all about my breathtaking Vera Wang gown (rumoured to have cost a five-figure sum), my celebrity guests (including the gay couple du jour, Cleo and Chelsea), and the decadent wedding feast. By special arrangement with Luke and his mates, no mention was made of the process server or the unauthorised video of my waters breaking at Fashion Week. However, there was a separate piece about once-leading publicist Diane Wilderstein, who'd suffered a nervous breakdown and tried to crash the wedding, breaking her ankle in the process. The report noted that she was now recuperating in the psychiatric wing of St Vincent's Hospital and receiving the very best care available. An anonymous donor had apparently come forward to pay for further rehab treatment for Wilderstein in a special facility in Far North Queensland when she was released from hospital.

Well, it was the very least Michael and I could do, seeing as Diane and her cohorts had given us a special day that would be talked about for years.

We were now setting off on a luxe honeymoon to the south of France and the Seychelles, and we were pleased to be able to help Diane out with her little sojourn to Far North Queensland. There was only one drawback to the clinic: the dry-out den was snake infested, with the operators reluctant to sort out this infestation since the aim was for all the patients to be at one with nature. Anyway, most of them were harmless carpet snakes, with only a few pythons and, very rarely, the odd deadly brown snake.

But, the way we looked at it, this was a good opportunity for Diane to tackle all her issues in one go, including her snake phobia. It was a delicious irony after all that the biggest snake in the PR world would get over all her addictions in a nest of vipers. And perhaps it would restore her to fight on for another day – who knows what miracles might occur.

Y

As for me, the honeymoon with Michael and Fifi (we couldn't leave her at home for that long, and Anna came along too) was both incredibly romantic and relaxing. This may have been because for two weeks I was banned from using my mobile or even glancing at my emails – although clearly something had shifted during this time.

I thought that when I returned there would be even more chaos, but the first thing I learnt was that the Russians had unexpectedly dropped the law suit (perhaps they had finally been convinced they stood to lose far more than they would gain). I still felt a little uneasy about this because it was not like Ivan and Svetlana to give up on anything. However, they were rumoured to have returned home (with more than a little help from the Department of Immigration). So I would have more time to devote to our projects, including Tod Spelsen's massive launch.

Looking back on that period of time now, everything had seemed almost unnaturally calm but we hadn't questioned it – we just got along with our lives as best we could. All that changed one afternoon when we all returned home at the same time. Fifi, Anna and I had been together at Queen Bee headquarters and Michael had insisted on picking us up. The plan was that we were going to put Fifi to bed and then leave her with Anna, while we went out for a quick bite to eat at Otto.

Usually we entered the house through the garage. I don't know what made me look into the front courtyard. But there, waiting for us on the doorstep, was a beautifully wrapped present with a card addressed to us in what looked like oddly familiar handwriting. I remember noticing the Selfridges logo which was visible beneath the wrapping paper and feeling slightly excited. It's funny the things that stick in your mind – like at the recent Myer show, remembering the freakin' cellulite on a model's thigh during a runway show and forgetting all about the label she was wearing.

Anyway, the reason that we didn't go to pick up the gift straight away is because it was so unexpected to find anything there. How had it been placed so pristinely in the doorway when it's almost impossible to get through the locked gate? How could anyone have lobbed the gift over the high wall and have it land like that?

Michael is always naturally suspicious, so he bent down to study the present without actually touching it. He put his ear to the box, signalling for us to be quiet. Then his face absolutely drained of colour. Lurching towards us – almost falling on top of us – he grabbed Fifi from a startled Anna's arms and herded us out into the street, bellowing out a single word which reverberated through my body, 'Run.'

STRICTLY CONFIDENTIAL

ROXY JACENKO

Meet Jasmine Lewis, the smart young publicist trying to work her way up from the bottom in Sydney's hottest PR company. She's done the coffee runs, the dry-cleaning pickups, the 5 a.m. starts, the 11 p.m. finishes. But still her evil boss Diane Wilderstein is never happy. So when Jasmine finds herself being summoned to Diane's office early one morning, she knows something's got to give. Luckily for Jasmine, fate lends a hand and helps her escape from the evil Diane to launch a fabulous new career.

That should be a dream come true, right? Or is it the start of a whole new world of nightmares?

'Ever wondered what really goes on behind the slick facade of the PR world? Strictly Confidential will knock your Manolos off!' Gemma Crisp, former editor of CLEO

ISBN 978 1 74237 757 5